THE MOGOLLON GUN-FIGHTER

"It's a grand feeling to be young and tough, with a heart full of hell, strong muscles, and quick hands. And the feeling that somewhere in the town ahead there's a man who would like to cut you down to size with hands or gun."

SILVER CANYON

Louis L'Amour's blazing story of Matt Brennan, one of the last of the great gun-fighters.

Bantam Books by Louis L'Amour
Ask your bookseller for the books you have missed

Louis L'Amour
Silver Canyon

BANTAM BOOKS
TORONTO · NEW YORK · LONDON

SILVER CANYON
A Bantam Book

PRINTING HISTORY

Published in a shorter version in GIANT WESTERN,
*June 1951, under the title "Riders of the Dawn,"
Copyright 1951 by Best Publications, Inc.*

Bouregy and Curl edition published October 1956

Bantam edition / November 1957

2nd printing .... January 1958	6th printing ...... April 1969
3rd printing .... July 1964	7th printing .... October 1969
4th printing .... June 1967	8th printing ..... March 1970
5th printing ... February 1969	9th printing .... July 1970

New Bantam edition / June 1971

2nd printing .... July 1971	6th printing .... January 1974
3rd printing .... March 1972	7th printing .... October 1974
4th printing .. September 1972	8th printing .... August 1975
5th printing ...... April 1973	9th printing .. December 1975
	10th printing .. February 1977

ISBN 0-553-10822-0

Published simultaneously in the United States and Canada

---

*Bantam Books are published by Bantam Books, Inc. Its trade-
mark consisting of the words "Bantam Books" and the por-
trayal of a bantam, is registered in the United States Patent
Office and in other countries. Marca Registrada. Bantam
Books, Inc., 666 Fifth Avenue, New York, New York 10019.*

PRINTED IN THE UNITED STATES OF AMERICA

SILVER CANYON

ONE

I RODE DOWN FROM THE HIGH BLUE hills and across the brush flats into Hattan's Point, a raw bit of spawning hell scattered hit or miss along the rocky slope of a rust-topped mesa.

This was the country for a man, a big country to grow in, a country where every man stood on his own feet and the wealth of a new land was his for the taking.

Ah, it's a grand feeling to be young and tough, with a heart full of hell, strong muscles, and quick hands! And the feeling that somewhere in the town ahead there's a man who would like to cut you down to size with hands or gun.

It was like that, Hattan's Point was, when I swung down from my buckskin. A new town, a new challenge; and if there were those who wished to try my hand, let them come and be damned.

I knew the raw whiskey of this town would be the raw whiskey of the last. But I shoved open the batwing doors and walked to the bar and took my glass of rye and downed it, then looked around to measure the men at the bar and the tables.

None of them were men whom I knew, yet I had seen their likes in a dozen towns back along the dusty trails I'd been riding since boyhood.

The big, hard-eyed rancher with the iron-gray hair, who thought he was the cock of the walk, and the lean, keen-faced man at his side with the careful eyes, who would be gun-slick and fast as a striking snake.

And there were the others there, men of the western melting pot, all of them looking for the pot of gold, and each of them probably a man to be reckoned with, and no one of them ready to admit himself second best to any. And me among them.

I remembered then what my old dad told me, back in the hills where I ate my first corn pone. "See it, lad. Live it. There'll never be its like again, not in our time nor any other."

He'd been west, he'd seen it growing out of the days of Bridges and Carson, seen the days of fur change to the day of buffalo, and finally to the day of beef cattle. He sent me west in my 'teens and told me I'd have to walk tall and cut a wide swath.

The big man with the iron-gray hair turned to me as a great brown bear turns to look at a squirrel.

"Who sent for you?"

There was harsh challenge in the words. The cold demand of a conqueror, and I laughed inside me. His voice lifted me to recklessness, for it was here, the old pattern I'd seen before, in other towns, far back down the trail.

"Nobody sent for me." I let a fine insolence come into my voice. "I ride where I want and stop when I wish."

He was a man grown used to smaller men who spoke respectfully, and my reply was an affront. His face went cold and still, but he thought me only an upstart then.

"Then ride on," he said. "You're not wanted in Hattan's Point."

"Sorry, friend, I like it here. Maybe in whatever game you're playing, I'll buy some chips."

His big face flushed, but before he could shape an answer, another man spoke. A tall young man with white hair.

"What he means is there's trouble here, and men

are taking sides. A man alone may be any man's enemy."

"Then maybe I'll choose a side," I said. "I always liked a fight."

The thin man was watching me, reading me, and he had a knowing eye, that one.

"Talk to me before you decide," he said.

"To you," I said, "or to any man."

When I went outside the sun was bright on the street. It had been cold on the bench where I'd slept last night, cold under the shadow of the ridge rising above me. The chill had been slow to leave and the sun now was warm to my flesh.

They would be speculating about me back there. I'd thrown down my challenge for pure fun. I cared about no one, anywhere. . . . And then suddenly I did.

She stood on the board walk before me, straight and slim and lovely, with a softly curved body and magnificent eyes, and hair of deepest black. Her skin was lightly tanned, her lips full and rich with promise.

My black chaps were dusty and worn, and my gray shirt sweat-stained from travel. My jaws were lean and unshaved, and under the tipped flat-brimmed hat my hair was black as hers, and rumpled. I was in no shape to meet a girl like that, but there she was, and in that instant I knew she was the girl for me, the only girl.

You can say it cannot happen, but it does, and it did. Back along the road there had been girls. Lightly I'd loved, and then passed on, but when I looked into the eyes of this girl I knew there would be no going on for me. Not tomorrow or next year, nor ten years from now. Unless this girl rode with me.

In two steps I was beside her, and the quick sound of my boots on the board walk turned her around sharply.

"I've nothing but a horse and the guns I wear," I

said quickly, "and I realize that my appearance is not one to arouse interest, let alone love, but this seemed the best time for you to meet the man you are to marry. The name is Mathieu Brennan."

Startled, as well she might be, it was a moment before she found words. They were angry words.

"Well, of all the egotistical—!"

"Those are kind words! More true romances have begun with those words than with any others. Now, if you will excuse me?"

I turned, put on my hat, and vaulting lightly over the rail, swung into the saddle.

She was standing as she had been, staring at me, her eyes astonished, but no longer quite so angry as curious.

"Good afternoon!" I lifted my hat. "I'll call on you later."

It was the time to leave. Had I attempted to push the acquaintance further I'd have gotten exactly nowhere, but now she would be curious, and there is no trait that women possess more fortunate for men.

The livery stable at Hattan's Point was a huge and rambling structure at the edge of town. From a bin I got a scoop of corn, and while my buckskin absorbed this warning against hard days to come, I curried him.

This was a job that had to be done with care. The buckskin liked it, but his nature was to protest, so I avoided his heels as I worked.

A jingle of spurs warned me and, glancing between my legs as I was bent over, I saw a man standing behind me, leaning against the stall post.

Straightening, I worked steadily for a full minute before I turned casually. Not knowing I had seen him, he was expecting me to be surprised.

The man was shabby and unkempt, but he wore two guns, the only man in town whom I'd seen wearing two guns except for the thin man in the saloon.

This one was tall and lean, and there was a tightness about his mouth I did not like.

"Hear you had a run-in with Rud Maclaren."

"No trouble."

"Folks say Canaval offered you a job."

Canaval? That would be the keen-faced man, the man with two guns. And Rud Maclaren the one who had ordered me from town. Absorbing this information, I made no answer.

"My name's Jim Pinder, CP outfit. I'll pay top wages, seventy a month an' found. All the ammunition you can use."

My eyes had gone beyond him where two men lurked in a dark stall, believing themselves unseen. They had come with Pinder, of that I was sure.

Suppose I refused Pinder's offer? Nothing about the setup looked good to me, and I could feel my hackles rising. The idea of him planting two men in the stall got under my skin.

Shoving Pinder aside, I stepped quickly into the open space between the stalls.

"You two!" My hands were over my guns and my voice rang loud in the echoing emptiness of the building. "Get out in the open! Move, or start shootin'!"

My hands were wide, my fingers spread, and right then I did not care which way the cat jumped. There was that old jumping devil in me that always boiled up to fight—not anger, exactly, nor any lust for killing but simply the urge to do battle that I'd known since I was a youngster.

There was a moment when I did not believe they would come out, a moment when I almost hoped they wouldn't. Jim Pinder had been caught flat-footed, and he didn't like what was happening. It was obvious to him that he would get a fast slug in the stomach if anything popped.

They came out then, slowly, holding their hands wide from their guns. They came with reluctance— more than half ready for battle, but not quite.

One of them was a big man with black hair and blue-black jowls. The other had the flat, cruel face of an Apache.

"Suppose we'd come shootin'?" The black-haired man was talking.

"Then they would have planted you before sundown." I smiled at him. "If you don't believe it, cut loose your wolf."

They did not know me and I was too ready. They were wise enough to see I'd been trailing with the rough-string but they didn't know how far I could carry my bluff.

"You move fast." Pinder was talking. "What if I had cut myself in?"

"I was expecting it." My smile angered him. "You would have gone first, then a quick one for Blackie, and after that"—I indicated the Apache—"him. He would be the hardest to kill."

Jim Pinder did not like it, and he did not like me. Nonetheless, he had a problem.

"I made an offer."

"And I'm turning it down."

His lips thinned down and I've seldom seen so much hatred in a man's eyes. I'd made him look small in front of his hired hands.

"Then get out. Join Maclaren and you'll die."

When you're young you can be cocky. I was young then and I was cocky, and I knew I should be wiser and hold my tongue. But I was feeling reckless and ready for trouble, and in no mood for beating around the greasewood.

"Then why wait," I threw it right in his teeth with a taunt. "So far as I know, I'm not joining Maclaren, but any time you want what I've got, come shootin'."

"You won't live long."

"No? Well, I've a hunch I'll stand by when they throw dirt on your face."

With that, I stepped to one side and looked at

Pinder. "You first, *amigo*, unless you'd like to make an issue."

He walked away from me, followed by his two men, and I waited and watched them go. I'll not deny I was relieved. With three men I'd have come out on the short end—but somebody would have gone with me and Jim Pinder was no gambler. Not right then, at least.

Up the street from the door of the stable I could see a welcome sign:

MOTHER O'HARA'S COOKING

MEALS FOUR-BITS

When I pushed open the door there were few at table—it was early for supper—but the young man with the white hair was eating, and beside him was the girl I loved.

It was a long, narrow, and low-ceilinged room of adobe, with white-washed walls, and it had the only plank floor among the town's three eating houses. The tables were neat, the dishes clean, and the food looked good. The girl looked up, and right away the light of battle came into her eyes. I grinned at her and bowed slightly.

The white-haired man looked at me, surprised, then glanced quickly at the girl, whose cheeks were showing color.

The buxom woman who came in from the kitchen stopped and looked from one to the other of us, then a smile flickered at the corner of her mouth. This, I correctly guessed, was Mother O'Hara. The girl returned to her eating without speaking.

The man spoke. "You've met Miss Maclaren then?"

Maclaren, was it?

"Not formally," I said, "but she's been on my mind for years." And knowing a valuable friend when I saw one, I added, "And it's no wonder she's lovely, if she eats here!"

"I can smell the blarney in that," Mother O'Hara said dryly, "but if it's food you want, sit down."

There was an empty bench opposite them, so I sat there. The girl did not look up, but the man offered his hand across the table. "I'm Key Chapin. And this, to make it formal, is Moira Maclaren."

"I'm Brennan," I said, "Matt Brennan."

A grizzled and dusty man from the far end of the table looked up. "Matt Brennan of Mobeetie, the Mogollon gunfighter?"

They all looked at me then, for it was a name not unknown. The reputation I'd rather not have had, but the name was mine and the reputation one I had earned.

"The gentleman knows me."

"Yet you refused Maclaren's offer?"

"And Pinder's , too."

They studied me, and after a minute Chapin said, "I'd have expected you to accept—one or the other."

"I play my own cards," I told him, "and my gun's not for hire."

TWO

MRS. O'HARA CAME IN WITH MY FOOD and I ate and drank coffee and let the others wait and think. Nor could I miss knowing what they were thinking of. In the past it had not mattered. I'd been a drifter, a man riding from town to town.

It was otherwise now ... suddenly. And the difference was a girl with green eyes and dark hair. I knew

I had been looking for her, for this girl across the table. And what I wanted to give her could not be bought with a gunfighter's wages.

The food was good and I ate heartily. They finished, but they sat over coffee. Finally I finished too, and began to build a smoke.

Where did I go from here? How did a man turn from the trail and settle down? For this was a girl who had a good home. I could offer her no less.

"What's the fight about?" I asked presently.

"What are most fights about? Sheep, cattle, or grass. Or water . . . and that's what it is in this case.

"East of here there's a long valley, Cottonwood Wash. Running into it from the east is Two-Bar Canyon. There's a good year-round stream flowing out of Two-Bar, enough to irrigate hay land or water thousands of cattle. Maclaren needs it, the C.P. wants it."

"Who's got it?"

"A man named Ball. He's no fighter, and he has no money to hire fighters. He hates Maclaren, and he refuses to do business with Pinder."

"And he's right in the middle."

Chapin put down his cup and took out his tobacco and pipe. "Gamblers in town are offering odds he won't last thirty days, even money he'll be killed within ten."

So that was the way of it? Two cow outfits wanting the water that another had. Two big outfits wanting to grow, and a little one holding them back.

No fighter was he? But a man with nerve . . . it took nerve to sit on the hot seat like that.

But that was enough for now. My eyes turned to the daughter of Rud Maclaren. "You can buy your trousseau," I said. "You'll not have long for planning."

She looked at me coolly, but there was impudence in her, too.

"I'll not worry about it. There's no weddings on Boot Hill."

They all laughed at that, yet behind it they were

all thinking she was right. When a man starts wearing a gun it is a thing to think about, but there was something inside me that told me no . . . not yet. Not by gun or horse or rolling river . . . not just yet.

"You've put your tongue to prophecy," I said, "and maybe it's in Boot Hill I'll end. But I'll tell you this, daughter of Maclaren, before I sleep in Boot Hill there will be sons and daughters of ours on this ground.

"I've a feeling on this, and mountain people set store by feelings. That when I go I'll be carried there by six tall sons of ours, and you'll be with them, remembering the good years we've had."

When the door slapped shut behind me I knew I'd been talking like a fool, yet the feeling was still with me—and why, after all, must it be foolishness?

Through the thin panels I heard Mother O'Hara telling her, "You'd better be buying that trousseau, Moira Maclaren! There's a lad knows his mind!"

"It's all talk," she said, "just loose talk."

She did not sound convinced, however, and that was the way we left it, for I knew there were things to be done.

Behind me were a lot of trails and a lot of rough times. Young as I was, I'd been a man before my time, riding with trail herds, fighting Comanches and rustlers, and packing a fast gun before I'd put a man's depth in my chest.

It was easy to talk, easy to make a boast to a pretty girl's ears, but I'd no threshold to carry her over, nor any land anywhere. It was a thought that had never bothered me before this, but when a man starts to think of a woman of his own, and of a home, he begins to know what it means to be a man.

Yet standing there in the street with the night air coming down from the hills, and darkness gathering itself under the barn eaves and along the streets, I found an answer.

It came to me suddenly, but the challenge of it set

my blood to leaping and brought laughter to my lips. For now I could see my way clear, my way to money, to a home, and to all I'd need to marry Moira Maclaren ... The way would be rough and bloody, but only the daring of it gripped my mind.

Turning, I started toward the stable, and then I stopped, for there was a man standing there.

He was a huge man, towering over my six feet two inches, broader and heavier by far than my two hundred pounds. He was big-boned and full of raw power, unbroken and brutal. He stood wide-legged before me, his face as wide as my two hands, his big head topped by a mass of tight curls.

"You're Brennan?"

"Why, yes," I said, and he hit me.

There was no start to the blow. His big balled fist hit my jaw like an axe butt and something seemed to slam me behind the knees and I felt myself falling. He hit me again as I fell into his fist, a wicked blow that turned me half around.

He dropped astride of me, all two hundred and sixty pounds of him, and with his knees pinning my arms, he aimed smashing, brutal blows at my head and face. Finally he got up, stepped back, and kicked me in the ribs.

"If you're conscious, hear me. I'm Morgan Park, and I'm the man who's boing to marry Moira Maclaren."

My lips were swollen and bloody and my brain foggy. "You lie!" I said, and he kicked me again and then walked away, whistling.

Somehow I rolled over and got my hands under me and pushed up to my knees. I crawled out of the street and against the stage station wall, where I lay with my head throbbing like a great drum, the blood welling from my split lips and broken face.

It had been a brutal beating he'd given me. I'd not been whipped since I was a boy, and never had I felt such blows as those. His fists had been like knots of oak and his arms like the limbs of trees.

Every breath I took brought a gasp, and I was sure he'd broken a rib for me. Yet it was time for me to travel. I'd made big talk in Hattan's Point and I'd not want Moira Maclaren to see me lying in the street like a whipped hound.

My hands found the corner of the building and I pulled myself up. Staggering along the building, using the wall for support, I made my way to the livery stable.

When I got my horse saddled, I pulled myself into the saddle and rode to the door.

The street was empty . . . no one had seen the beating I'd taken, and wherever Morgan Park had come from, now he was nowhere to be seen. For an instant I sat my horse in the light of the lantern above the stable floor.

A door opened and a shaft of light fell across me. In the open door of Mother O'Hara's stood Moira Maclaren.

She stepped down from the stoop and walked over to me, looking up at my swollen and bloody face with a kind of awed wonder.

"So he found you, then. He always hears when anyone comes near me, and this always happens. You see, Matt, it is not so simple a thing to marry Moira Maclaren." There seemed almost a note of regret in her voice.

"And now you're leaving?" she said.

"I'll be back for you . . . and to give Morgan Park a beating."

Now her voice was cool, shaded with contempt. "You boast—all you have done is talk and take a beating!"

That made me grin, and the grinning hurt my face. "It's a bad beginning, isn't it?"

She stood there watching as I rode away down the street.

Throughout the night I rode into wilder and wilder country. I was like a dog hunting a hole in which to die, but I'd no thought of dying, only of living and finding Morgan Park again.

Through the long night I rode, my skull pounding, my aching body heavy with weariness, my face swollen and shapeless. Great canyon walls towered above me, and I drank of their coolness. Then I emerged on a high plateau where a long wind stole softly across the open levels fresh with sage and sego lilies.

Vaguely I knew the land into which I rode was a lost and lonely land inhabited by few, and those few were men who did not welcome visitors.

At daylight I found myself in a long canyon where tall pines grew. There was a stream talking somewhere under the trees, and, turning from the game trail I had followed, I walked my buckskin through knee-high grass and flowers and into the pines. It smelled good there, and I was glad to be alone in the wilderness which is the source of all strength.

There beside the stream I bedded down, opening my soogan and spreading it in the half sunlight and shade, and then I picketed my horse and at last crept to my blankets and relaxed with a great sigh. And then I slept.

It was midafternoon when my eyes opened again. There was no sound but the stream and the wind in the tall pines, a far-off, lonely sound. Downstream a beaver splashed, and in the trees a magpie chattered, fussing at a squirrel.

I was alone. ... With small sticks I built a fire and heated water, and when it was hot I bathed my face with careful hands, and while I did it I thought of the man who had whipped me.

It was true he had slugged me without warning, then had pinned me down so I'd have no chance to escape from his great weight. But I had to admit I'd been whipped soundly. Yet I wanted to go back. This was not a matter for guns. This man I must whip with my bare hands.

But there was much else to consider. From all I had learned, the Two-Bar was the key to the situation, and it had been my idea to join forces with Ball, the man who was stubborn enough to face up to two strong outfits. I'd long had an urge for lost causes, and a feeling for men strong enough to stand alone. If Ball would have my help . . .

To the west of where I waited was a gigantic cliff rising sheer from the grassy meadow. Trees skirted the meadow, and to the east a stream flowed along one side, where the pines gave way to sycamore and a few pin oak.

Twice I saw deer moving among the trees. Lying in wait near the water, I finally got my shot and dropped a young buck.

For two days I ate, slept, and let the stream flow by. My side ceased to pain except when a sudden movement jerked it, but it remained stiff and sore to the touch. The discoloration around my eyes and on one cheekbone changed color and some of the swelling went down. After two days I could wait no longer. Mounting the buckskin, I turned him toward the Two-Bar.

A noontime sun was darkening the buckskin with sweat when I turned into Cottonwood Wash.

There was green grass here, and there were trees and water. The walls of the Wash were high and the trees towered until their tops were level with them, occasional cattle I saw looked fat and lazy.

For an hour I rode slowly along, feeling the hot sun on my shoulders and smelling the fresh green of the grass, until the trail ended abruptly at a gate bearing a large sign.

TWO-BAR GATE

RANGED FOR A SPENCER .56

SHOOTING GOING ON HERE

Beyond this point a man would be taking his own chances, and nobody could say he had not been warned.

Some distance away, atop a knoll, I could see the house. Rising in my stirrups, I waved my hat. Instantly there was the hard *whap* of a bullet passing, then the boom of the rifle.

Obviously, this was merely a warning shot, so I waved once more.

That time the bullet was close, so, grabbing my chest with both hands I rolled from the saddle, caught the stirrup to break my fall and settled down to the grass. Then I rolled over behind a boulder. Removing my hat, I sailed it to the ground near the horse, then pulled off one boot and placed it on the ground so it would be visible from the gate. But from that far away an observer would see only the boot, not whether there was a foot and leg attached.

Then I crawled into the brush, among the rocks, where I could cover the gate. To all outward appearances a man lay sprawled behind that boulder.

All was still. Sweat trickled down my face. My side throbbed a little from a twist it had taken as I fell from the horse. I dried my sweaty palms and waited.

And then Ball appeared. He was a tall old man with a white handlebar mustache and shrewd eyes. No fool, he studied the layout carefully, and he did not like it. It looked as though he had miscalculated and scored a hit.

He glanced at the strange brand of the buckskin, at the California bridle and bit. Finally, he opened the gate and came out, and as he turned his back was to me.

"Freeze, Ball! You're dead in my sights!"

He stood perfectly still, taking no chances on an itchy trigger finger.

"Who are you? What do you want with me?"

"Not trouble ... I want to talk business."

"I've no business with anybody."

"With me you've business. I'm Matt Brennan. I've had trouble with Pinder and Maclaren. I've taken a beating from Morgan Park."

Ball chuckled. "Sounds as if you're the one with trouble. Is it all right to turn around?"

At my word, he turned. I stepped from out of the rocks. He moved back far enough to see the boot and grinned. "I'll not bite on that one again."

I sat down and pulled my boot on.

THREE

WHEN I WAS ON MY FEET I CROSSED TO my hat and picked it up. He watched me, never letting his eyes leave me for an instant.

"You're bucking a stacked deck," I said. "The gamblers are offering high odds you won't last thirty days."

"I know that."

He was a hard old man, this one. Yet I could see from the fine lines around his eyes that he'd been missing sleep, and that he was worried. But he wasn't frightened. Not this man.

"I'm through drifting. I'm going to put down some roots, and there's only one ranch around here I'd have."

"This one?"

"Yes."

He studied me, his hands on his hips. I'd no doubt he would go for a gun if I made a wrong move.

"What do you aim to do about me?"

"Let's walk up to your place and talk about that."

"We'll talk here."

"All right. . . . There's two ways. You give me a fighting, working partnership. That's one way. The other is for you to sell out to me and I'll pay you when I can. I take over the fight."

He looked at me carefully. He was not a man to ask foolish questions. He could see the marks of the beating I'd taken, and he'd heard me say there had been trouble with Maclaren and Pinder. I knew what I was asking for.

"Come on up. We'll talk about this."

And he let me go first, leading my horse. I liked this old man.

Yet I knew the cards were stacked my way. He could not stay awake all night, every night. He could not both work and guard his stock. He could not go to town for supplies and leave the place unguarded. Together we could do all those things.

Two hours later we had reached an agreement. I was getting my fighting, working partnership. One man alone could not do it, the odds were all against any two men doing it . . . but they'd have a chance.

"When they find out, they'll be fit to be tied."

"They won't find out right away. My first job is grub and ammunition."

The Two-Bar controlled most of the length of Cottonwood Wash and on its eastern side opened upon a desert wilderness with only occasional patches of grass. Maclaren's Boxed M and Pinder's CP bordered the ranch on the west, with Maclaren's land extending to the desert at one place.

Both ranches had pushed back the Two-Bar cattle, usurping the range for their own use. In the process, most of the Two-Bar calves had disappeared under Boxed M and CP brands.

"Mostly CP," Ball advised. "The Pinder boys are mighty mean. They rode with Quantrill, an' folks say

Rollie rode with the James boys some. Jim's a fast gun, but nothin' to compare to Rollie."

At daybreak, with three unbranded mules to carry the supplies, I started for Hattan's, circling wide around so that I could come into the trail to town from the side opposite the Two-Bar.

It was in my mind that the Two-Bar might be watched, but after scouting the edges of the Wash I decided that they must believe they had Ball safely bottled up and no chance of his getting help. Probably they would be only too glad for him to start to town ... for when he returned they could be in possession and waiting for him.

Going down the Wash for several miles, I came out by a narrow, unused trail and cut across country, keeping to low country to escape observation.

The desert greasewood gave way to mesquite and to bunch grass. The morning was bright, and the sun would be warm again. Twice, nearing the skyline, I saw riders in the distance, but none of them could have seen me.

The town was quiet when I rode in, and I came up through the shacks back of the livery stable and left my mules tied to the corral near the back door of the store.

Walking out on the street, I smoked a cigarette and kept my eyes open. Nobody seemed to notice me, nobody seemed to know I was in town. There was no sign of Maclaren or Canaval, or of Moira.

Loading the supplies, I broke into a sweat. The day was warm and still, and my side still pained me. My face was puffed, although both my eyes were now open and the blackness had changed to mottled blue and yellow. When I was through I led the mules into the cottonwoods on the edge of town and picketed them there, ready for a quick move. Then I returned to Mother O'Hara's. My purpose was double. I wanted a good meal, and I wanted news.

Key Chapin and Canaval were there and they

looked up as I entered. Chapin's eyes took in my face with a quick glance, and there was in his eyes something that might have been sympathy.

Canaval noticed, but it did not show. "That job is still open," he suggested. "We could use you."

"Thanks." There was a bit of recklessness in me. My supplies were packed and ready to go, and there was enough on those mules to last us three months, with a little game shooting on the side and a slaughtered beef or two. "I'm going to run my own outfit."

Maybe I was a fool to say it. Maybe I should have kept it a secret as long as I could. But just as I started to speak I heard a door open behind me and that light step and the perfume I knew. Maybe that was why I was here, to see Moira, and not for a meal or news.

From the day I first saw her she was never to be near without my knowledge. There was something within me that told me, some feeling in my blood, some perception beyond the usual. This was my woman, and I knew it.

She had come into the restaurant behind me and it may have been that that made me say it, to let her know that I had not cut and run, that I intended to stay, that I had begun to build for the future I had promised her.

"Your own outfit?" Chapin was surprised. "You're turning nester?"

Canaval said nothing at all, but he looked at me, and I think he knew then. I saw dawning comprehension in his eyes, and perhaps something of respect.

"I'll be ranching."

Rising, I faced around. Moira was looking at me, her eyes level and steady.

"Miss Maclaren?" I indicated the seat beside me. "May I have the pleasure?"

She hesitated, then shook her head slightly and went around the table to sit down beside Canaval, her father's foreman and strong right hand.

"You're *ranching?*" Canaval was puzzled. "If there's any open range around here I haven't heard of it."

"It's a place east of here . . . the Two-Bar."

"What about the Two-Bar?" Rud Maclaren had followed his daughter into the restaurant. He rounded the table beside her and looked down at me, a cold, solid man.

Taking a cup from a tray, I filled it with coffee.

"Mr. Brennan was telling us, Father, that he's ranching on the Two-Bar."

"*What?*"

Maclaren looked as if he'd been slapped.

"Ball needed help, and I wanted a ranch. I've a working partnership." Then looking up at Moira, I added, "And a man doesn't want to go too far from the girl he is to marry."

"What's that?" Maclaren was confused.

"Why, Father!" Moira's eyes widened, and a flicker of deviltry danced in them, "Haven't you heard? Mr. Brennan has been saying that he is going to marry me!"

"I'll see him in hell first!" He stared down at me. "Young man, you stop using my daughter's name or you'll face me."

"I'd rather not face you. I want to keep peace in the family." I lifted my cup and took a swallow of coffee. "Nobody has a greater respect for your daughter's name than I. After all . . . she is to be my wife."

Maclaren's face flushed angrily, but Canaval chuckled and even Moira seemed amused.

Key Chapin put in a quieting word before Maclaren could say what might have precipitated trouble.

"There's an aspect of this situation, Rud, that may have escaped you. If Brennan is now Ball's partner, it might be better to let him stay on, then buy him out."

Maclaren absorbed the idea and was pleased. It

was there in his eyes, plain to be seen. He looked down at me with new interest."

"Yes, yes, of course. We might do business, young man."

"We might . . . and we want peace, not trouble. But I did not become a partner to sell out. Also, in all honesty, I took on the partnership only by promising never to sell. Tomorrow I shall choose a building site.

"Which brings up another point. There are Boxed M cattle on Two-Bar range. It should take you no longer than a week to remove them. I shall inform the CP of the same time limit."

Maclaren's face was a study. He started to speak, then hesitated. Finishing my coffee, I got to my feet, I put down a coin and went out the door, closing it softly just as Maclaren started to speak.

There was a time for all things, and this was the time to leave . . . while I was ahead.

Rounding the building, I brought up short. Pinder's black-haired rider was standing beside my horse. There was a gun in his hand and an ugly look in his eyes.

"You talk too much. I heard that you'd moved in with Ball."

"So you heard."

"Sure, and Jim will pay a bonus for your hide."

His finger tightened and I threw myself aside and palmed my gun. It was fast . . . the instinctive reaction of a man trained to use a gun. The gun sprang to my hand, it bucked in my palm. I heard the short, heavy bark of it, and between my first and second shots, his gun slammed a bullet that drew blood from my neck.

Blackie turned as if to walk away, then fell flat, his fingers clawing hard at the dirt.

Men came rushing among them those from Mother O'Hara's. "Seen it!" The speaker was a short, leather-faced man who had been harnessing a horse in the

alley near by. "Blackie laid for him with a drawn
gun."

Canaval's gaze was cool, attentive. "A drawn gun?
That was fast, man."

Maclaren looked at me more carefully. Probably he
had believed I was some fresh youngster, but now he
knew that I'd used a gun. This was going to change
things. Instead of one lonely old man on the Two-Bar
there was now another man, a young man, one who
could shoot fast and straight.

When I could, I backed from the crowd and went
to my horse, leading him around the corner into the
street. Stepping into the leather, I looked around and
saw Moira on the steps, watching me. I lifted my hat,
then cantered away to the cottonwoods and my mules.

Ball was at the gate when I arrived, and I could
see the relief in his eyes.

"Trouble?"

My account was brief, and to the point. There was
nothing about killing that I liked.

"One more," Ball said grimly, "and one less."

But I was remembering the face of the girl on the
steps. Moira knew now that I'd killed a man. How
would she feel about that? How would she look upon
me now?

FOUR

DURING THE NEXT TWO DAYS I SPENT
hours in the saddle going over the lands that lay under the Two-Bar brand. It was even better than I had
expected, and it was easy to see why the CP and the
Boxed M were envious.

Aside from the rich grass of Cottonwood Wash, and the plentiful water supply, there were miles of bunch grass country before the desert was reached, and even the desert was rich in a growth of antelope bush and wool fat.

It was a good ranch, with several waterholes other than the stream along the Wash, and with sub-irrigation over against the mountains. Only to the west were there ranches, and only from the west could other cattle get into the area to mingle with the Two-Bar herd.

Ball's calves had largely been rustled by the large outfits, and if we expected to prosper we must rid ourselves of the stock we had and get some young stuff. The cattle we had would never be in any better shape, but from now on would grow older and tougher. Now was the time to sell yet a drive was impossible.

Ball was frankly discouraged. "I'm afraid they've got us bottled up, Matt," he told me. "When you came along I was about ready to cash in my chips."

"Outfit down in the hills past Organ Rock."

Ball's head lifted sharply. "Forgot to tell you. Stay clear of that bunch. That's the Benaras place, the B Bar B. Six in the family. They have no truck with anybody—an' all of them are dead shots."

He smoked in silence for a while, and I considered the situation on the ranch. There was no time to be lost, and no sense in being buffaloed. The thing to do was to start building the outfit now.

An idea had come to my mind, and when I saddled up the next morning I drifted south.

It was a wild and lonely country, toward Organ Rock. Furrowed and eroded by thousands of years of sun, wind, and rain, a country tumbled and broken as if by some insane giant. Miles of raw land with only occasional spots of green to break the everlasting reds, pinks, and whites.

Occasionally, in the midst of a barren and lonely

stretch, there would be an oasis of green, with trees, water, and grass. At each of these would be a few cattle, fat and lazy under the trees.

A narrow trail led up to the mesa, and I took it, letting the buckskin find his own way. There were few horse tracks, which told me that even the boys from the B Bar B rarely came this far.

Wind moved across the lonely mesa, the junipers stirred. I drew up, standing in the half shade of the tree and looking ahead. The mesa seemed empty, yet I had a sudden feeling of being observed. For a long time I listened, but no sound came across the silences.

The buckskin walked on, almost of his own volition. Another trail intersected, a more traveled trail. Both led in the direction I was now taking.

There was no sound but the footfalls of my horse, the lonely creak of the saddle, and once, far off, the cry of an eagle. A rabbit bounded up and away bouncing like a tufted rubber ball.

The mesa broke off sharply and before me lay a green valley not unlike Cottonwood Wash, but far wilder and more remote. Towering rock walls skirted it, and a dark-mouthed canyon opened wide into the valley. The trail down from the mesa led from bench to bench with easy swings and switchbacks, and I descended, riding more warily.

Twice antelope appeared in the distance and once a deer. There were tracks of cattle, but few were in evidence.

The wild country to the east, on my left, was exciting to see. A vast maze of winding canyons and broken ledges, of towering spires and massive battlements. It was a land unexplored and unknown, and greatly tempting to an itching foot.

A click of a drawn-back hammer stopped me in my tracks. Buck stood perfectly still, his ears up, and I kept both hands on the pommel.

"Goin' somewhar, stranger?"

The voice seemed to come from a clump of boulders at the edge of a hay meadow, but there was nobody in sight.

"I'm looking for the boss of the B Bar B."

"What might you want with him?"

"Business talk. I'm friendly."

The chuckle was dry. "Ever see a man covered by two Spencers who wasn't friendly?"

The next was a girl's voice. "Who you ridin' fo'?"

"I'm Matt Brennan, half-owner of the Two-Bar."

"You could be lyin'."

"Do I see the boss?"

"I reckon."

A tall boy of eighteen stepped from the rocks. Lean and loose-limbed, he looked tough and wise beyond his years. He carried his Spencer as if it was part of him. He motioned with his head to indicate a trail into the wide canyon.

Light steps came from somewhere behind him as he walked the buckskin forward. He did not turn in the saddle and kept his hands in sight.

The old man of the tribe was standing in front of a stone house built like a fort. Tall as his sons who stood beside him, he was straight as a lodge-pole pine.

To right and left, built back near the rock walls, were stables and other buildings. The hard-packed earth was swept clean, the horses were curried, and all the buildings were in good shape. Whatever else the Benaras family might be, they were workers.

The old man looked me over without expression. Then he took the pipe from his lean jaws.

"Get down an' set."

Inside, the house was as neat as on the outside. The floors were freshly scrubbed, as was the table. Nor was there anything makeshift about it. The house and furniture had been put together by skillful hands, each article shaped with care and affection.

A stout, motherly-looking woman put out cups and poured coffee. A girl in a neat cotton dress brought home-baked bread and home-made butter to the table. Then she put out a pot of honey.

"Our own bees." Old Bob Benaras stared from under shaggy brows. He looked like a patriarch right out of the Bible.

He watched me as I talked, smoking quietly. I ate a slice of bread, and did not spare the butter and honey. He watched with approval, and the girl brought a tall glass filled with creamy milk.

"We've some fat stock," I told him, "but we can't make a drive. What I would like is to trade the grown cattle to you, even up, for some of your young stuff."

I drank half the milk and put the glass down. It had been cold, fresh-taken from a cave, no doubt.

"You can make your drive," I went on, "and you can sell, so you will lose nothing. It would be right neighborly."

He looked sharp at me when I used the word, and I knew at once it had been the right one. This fierce old man, independent and proud, respected family and neighbors.

"We'll swap." He knocked out his pipe. "My boys will help you round up and drive."

"No need—no reason you should get involved in this fight."

He turned those fierce blue eyes at me. "I'm buyin' cows," he said grimly. "Anybody who wants trouble over that can have it!"

"Now, Pa!" Mother Benaras smiled at me. "Pa figures he's still a-feudin'."

Benaras shook his head, buttering a slice of bread. "We're beholden to no man, nor will we backwater for any man. Nick, you roust out and get Zeb. Then saddle up and ride with this man. You ride to his orders. Start no trouble, but back up for nobody. Understand?"

Nick turned and left the room, and Benaras turned to his wife.

"Ma, set up the table. We've a guest in the house."
He looked at me, searchingly. "You had trouble with
Pinder yet?"

So I told him how it began, of the talk in the
stable, and of my meeting with Blackie later. I told
that in few words, saying only, "Blackie braced me
. . . waited for me with a drawn gun."

That was all I told them. The boys exchanged
looks, and the old man began to tamp tobacco in his
pipe.

"Had it comin'," that one. Jolly had trouble with him,
figured to kill him soon or late."

They needed no further explanation than that. A
man waited for you with a gun in hand . . . it followed
as the night the day that if you were alive the other
man was not. It also followed that you must have got
into action mighty fast.

It was a pleasant meal—great heaps of mashed pota-
toes, slabs of beef and venison, and several vegeta-
bles. All the boys were there, tall, lean, and alike
except for years. And all were carbon copies or their
hard-bitten old father.

Reluctantly, when the meal was over, I got up to
leave. Old Bob Benaras walked with me to my horse.
He put a hand on the animal and nodded.

"Know a man by his horse," he said, "or his gun.
Like to see 'em well chosen, well kept. You come
over, son, you come over just any time. We don't
neighbor much, ain't our sort of folks hereabouts. But
you come along when you like."

It was well after dark when we moved out, taking
our time, and knowing each one of us, that we might
run into trouble before we reached home. It was
scarcely within the realm of possibility that my leave-
taking had gone unobserved. Anxious as I was, I kept
telling myself the old man had been on that ranch
long before I appeared, that he could take care of
himself.

Remembering the sign on the gate, I felt better. No man would willingly face that Spencer.

The moon came out, and the stars. The heat of the day vanished, as it always must in the desert where there is no growth to hold it, only the bare rocks and sand. The air was thin on the high mesa and we speeded up, anxious to be home.

Once, far off, we thought we heard a sound ... Listening, we heard nothing.

At the gate I swung to open it, ready for a challenge.

Suddenly, Nick Benaras whispered, "Hold it!"

We froze, listening. We heard the sound of moving horses, and on the rim of the Wash, not fifty yards off, two riders appeared. We waited, rifles in our hands, but after a brief pause, apparently to listen, the two rode off toward town.

We rode through the gate and closed it. There was no challenge.

Zeb drew up sharply. "Nick!"

We stopped, waiting, listening.

"What is it, Zeb?"

"Smoke ... I smell smoke."

FIVE

FEAR WENT THROUGH ME LIKE A HOT blade. Slapping the spurs to my tired buckskin, I put the horse up the trail at a dead run, Nick and Zeb right behind me.

Then I saw the flicker of flames and, racing up, drew rein sharply.

The house was a charred ruin, with only a few

flames still flickering. The barn was gone, the corrals had been pulled down.

"Ball!" I yelled it, panic rising in me. "Ball!"

And above the feeble sound of flames I heard a faint cry.

He was hidden in a niche of rock near the spring, and the miracle was that he had lived long enough to tell his story. Fairly riddled with bullets, his clothes were charred and his legs had been badly burned. It took only a glance to know the old man was dying . . . there was no chance, none at all.

Behind me I heard Nick's sharp-drawn breath, and Zeb swore with bitter feeling.

Ball's fierce old eyes pleaded with me. "Don't . . . don't let 'em git the place! Don't . . . never!"

His eyes went beyond me to Nick and Zeb. "You witness. His now. I leave all I have to Matt . . . to Brennan. Never to sell! Never to give up!"

"Who was it?"

Down on my knees beside the old man, I came to realize the affection I'd had for him. Only a few days had we been together, but they had been good days, and there had been rare understanding between us. And he was going, shot down and left for dead in a burning house. For the first time I wanted to kill.

I wanted it so that my hands shook and my voice trembled. I wanted it so that the tears in my eyes were there as much from anger as from sorrow.

"Pinder!" His voice was only a hoarse whisper. "Rollie Pinder, he . . . was dressed like . . . you. I let him in, then . . . Strange thing . . . thought I saw Park."

"Morgan Park?" I was incredulous.

His lips stirred, trying to shape words, but the words would not take form. He looked up at me, and he tried to smile. . . . He died that way, lying there on the ground with the fire-light flickering on his face, and a cold wind coming along from the hills.

"Did you hear him say that Park was among them?"

"Ain't reasonable. He's thick with the Maclarens."

The light had been bad, Ball undoubtedly had been mistaken. Yet I made a mental reservation to check on Morgan Park's whereabouts.

The fire burned low and the night moved in with more clouds, shutting out the stars and gathering rich and black in the canyons. Occasional sparks flew up, and there was the smell of smoke and charred wood.

A ranch had been given me, but I had lost a friend. The road before me now stretched long and lonely, a road I must walk with my gun in my hand.

Standing there in the darkness, I made a vow that if there was no law here to punish the Pinders, and I knew no move would be made against them, I'd take the law in my own hand. Rollie would die and Jim would die, and every man who rode with them would live to rue that day.

And to the Benaras boys I said as much. They nodded, knowing how I felt. They were young men from a land of feud, men of strong friendship and bitter hatred, and of fights to the end.

"He was a good man," Zeb said. "Pa liked him."

For two days we combed the draws, gathering cattle. At the end of the second day we had only three hundred head. Rustling by the big brands had sadly depleted the herds of the Two-Bar.

We made our gather in the bottom of Cottonwood Wash, where there was water and grass. Once in that bottom, it was easy to hold the cows.

"Come morning, we'll start our drive."

Nick looked around at me. "Figure to leave the ranch unguarded?"

"If they move in," I told him, "they can move out again or be buried there."

The canyon channeled the drive and the cattle were in good shape and easy to handle. It took us all day to make the drive, skirting the mesa I had crossed in my first ride to Organ Rock. My side pained me very little although it was still stiff. There was only that gnawing, deep-burning anger at the killers of old man Ball to worry me.

They had left a wounded man to burn. They had killed a man who wanted only peace, the right to enjoy the ranch he had built from nothing. He had been an old man, strong for his years, but with a weariness on him and the need for quiet evenings and brisk, cool mornings, and a chair on a porch. And that old man had died in the falling timbers of his burning home, his body twisted with the pain of bullet wounds.

At the ranch we told our story to Benaras, and as he listened his hard old face stiffened with anger.

We ate there, sitting again at that table that seemed always heavy with food, and we talked long, saying nothing of what was to come, for we were men without threats. We were men who talked little of the deeds to be done.

Looking back over the few days since I had first come to Hattan's Point, I knew I had changed.

It is the right of youth to be gay and proud, to ride with a challenge. The young bull must always try his strength. It was always so, the test of strength and the test of youth. Yet when the male met his woman it was different. I had met mine thus, and I had seen an old man die . . . these are things to bring years to a man.

When day came again to Organ Rock, Jolly and Jonathan Benaras helped me start the herd of young stuff back up the trail. Benaras had given me two dozen head more than I'd asked in trade, but the stock I'd given him were heavy and ready for market as they stood.

Jolly had been at Hattan's when the news of the raid reached the town. The Apache trailer, Bunt Wilson, and Corby Kitchen had been on the raid, and three others unnamed.

"Hear anything said about Morgan Park?"

"Not him. Lyell, who rides for Park, he was along."

Ball might have meant to say it was a rider of Park's rather than Park himself. That was more likely.

Jonathan rode back from the point. He had gone on ahead, scouting the way.

"Folks at your place . . . two, maybe three."

Something in me turned cold and ugly. "Bring the herd. I'll ride on ahead."

Jonathan's big Adam's apple bobbed. "Jolly an' me, we ain't had much fun lately. Can't we come along?"

"Foot of the hill. Right below where the house was.

An idea hit me. "Where's their camp?"

They got them a tent."

"We'll take the herd . . . drive it right over the tent."

Jonathan looked at Jolly. "Boys'll be sore. Missin' all the fun."

We started the herd. They were young stuff and full of ginger, ready to run. They came out of the canyon some two hundred yards from the camp, and then we really lit into them.

With a wild yell, I banged a couple of quick shots from my gun and the herd lit out as if they were making a break for water after a long dry drive. They hit that stretch with their bellies to the grass and ran like deer.

Up ahead we saw men jumping up. Somebody yelled, somebody else grabbed for a rifle, and then that herd hit them, running full tilt.

One man dove for his horse, missed his grab, and fell sprawling. He came up running and just barely made it to the top of a rock as the herd broke around it.

The tent was smashed down, the food trampled into the dust. The fire scattered, utensils smashed and banged around. The herd went on through, some of them going up the hill, some breaking around it. The camp was a shambles, the gear the men had packed up there was ruined.

One man who had scrambled into a saddle in time swung his horse and came back. He was a big redhead and he looked tough. He was fighting mad.

"What goes on here? What the hell's this?"

He rode a Boxed M horse. Rud Maclaren's men had beaten the CP to the ranch.

Kneeing my horse alongside his, I told him. "I'm Matt Brennan, owner of the Two-Bar, with witnesses to prove it. You're trespassing. Now light a shuck!"

"I will like hell!" His face flushed with anger. "I got my orders, an' I—"

My fist backhanded into his teeth, smashing his lips to pulp. He went back out of the saddle and I swung my horse around and jumped to the ground as he started to get up. I hit him getting off the ground and he went down hard. He started up again, Then dove at my feet. I jumped back and as he sprawled out I grabbed his hair and jerked him up. I smashed a fist into his wind, and then shoved him off and hit him in the face with both hands. He went down, and he didn't make any move to get up.

Jonathan and Jolly had rounded up two more men and herded them to me.

One was a slim, hard-faced youngster who looked as if the devil was riding him. His kind I had seen before. The other was a stocky redhead with a scar on his jaw.

"You ruined my outfit," he said. "What kind of a deal is this?"

"When you ride for a fighting brand you can expect trouble. What did you expect when you came up here? A pink tea party? You go back and tell Maclaren not to send boys to do a man's job. I'll shoot the next trespasser on sight."

The younger one was sneering. "What if he sends

me?" He put his hands on his hips. "If I hadn't lost my gun in the scramble you'd eat that!"

"Jolly! Lend me your gun!"

Without a word, Benaras passed his six shooter to me.

The youngster's eyes were suddenly calculating and wary. He suspected a trick, but could not guess what it would be.

Taking the gun by the barrel, I walked toward him. "You get your chance," I said. Flipping it in my hand so the butt was up, I held it out. "Anyway you like. Try a border roll or shoot from where it is. Anyway you try it, I'm going to kill you."

He didn't like it. He stared at me and then at the gun. His tongue touched his lips. He wanted that gun so bad he could taste it, and my gun was in my holster.

He had that streak of viciousness it takes to make a killer, but suddenly he was face to face with killing and right now he wanted no part of it. The thing that bothered him was the fact that I'd gamble. No man would make such a gamble unless he knew . . . or unless he was crazy.

"It's a trick," he said. "You ain't that much of a fool."

"*Fool?*" That brought my fury surging to the top. "Why, you cheap, phony, imitation of a badman! I'd give you two guns and shoot your ears off any day you'd like!

"Right now! Shove your gun in my belly and I'll shove mine in yours! If you want to die, let's make it easy! Come on, you cheapskate! *Try it!*"

Crazy? Sure. But right then I didn't care. His face turned whiter and his eyes were hot and ugly. He was trembling with eagerness to grab that gun. But face to face? Guns shoved against the body? We would both die. We couldn't miss. He shook his head, and his lips were dry and his eyes staring.

"No . . . no. . . ."

My fingers held the gun by the barrel. Flipping it up, I caught the gun by the butt and dashed it down across his skull. He hit the dirt at my feet, knocked cold.

The two redheads were both on their feet staring at me, waiting.

"All right," I said. "Pick him up and get off the place."

"It was orders."

"You could quit, couldn't you?"

The stocky redhead stared at me. "He'll be huntin' you now. You won't live long. You know what that is?" He indicated the youngster on the ground. "That's Bodie Miller!"

The name was familiar. Bodie Miller had killed two men. He was known to be utterly vicious, and although he lacked seasoning he had it in him to be one of the worst.

The two redheads picked Miller off the ground and hoisted him into his saddle. Disarmed, they slowly walked their horses out of the Wash and took the trail for home.

The cattle were no cause for worry. They would not leave the good grass of the Wash nor of the feeder canyons from the east.

Jonathan Benaras rolled a smoke and hitched his one gallus higher on his shoulder after he had put the cigarette between his lips. He struck a match and lighted up.

"Well," he said wryly, "they cain't say you don't walk in swingin'. You've tackled nigh ever'body in the country!"

When they were gone, riding home and talking about it, I studied the situation. There was nothing about it that I liked. Maclaren would be back . . . or the Pinders would come, and I was one man alone.

SIX

It was no longer possible to defend the Two-Bar. No other decision was possible. Reluctantly, I decided that for the time, at least, I must have another place of retreat. Although I might remain at the ranch, I must be prepared to leave at an instant's notice.

Before Ball was killed we had made plans for our last stand, if that became necessary, at an old cliff house in Two-Bar canyon. Ball and I had stored some food there, and now, digging around in the ruins, I found some undamaged canned stuff that I transported up there and concealed near the cliff house.

As I rode I tried to think a way out of the corner in which I found myself.

My only friends were the Benaras family, but this was not their fight, it was mine.

Across the east was broken country of canyons and desert, almost without water, a country brutal and heat-blistered, where a man might die under a blazing sun, choking with thirst . . . unless he knew the waterholes.

On the west were the holdings of the CP and the Boxed M.

Once, not many weeks ago, I would have been tempted to start hunting down the men who had killed my partner. Now I knew better.

The way to defeat them was to hold the ranch, to keep it for myself, as Ball had wished, to keep them from what they had hoped to gain by murder. To do this I must stay alive, I must think, plan.

Now young cattle ran on Two-Bar grass. The

would be growing, fattening up. That much was done. But a new house must be built, new corrals. I must put down such solid roots that I could never be dislodged. And to have roots was a new thing for me.

Maclaren would, when possible, try to give the cover of right and legality to his actions. Pinder was under no such compulsion. Yet they were equally dangerous.

Another thing. I must keep the good will of those few friends I had. The Benaras family were really all. But at Hattan's Point there were people who, if not my friends, were not my enemies either. Key Chapin was not taking sides. Morally at least, I must have him on my side. Mrs. O'Hara was another.

Sheriff Tharp would not interfere in any ranch squabble. That Ball had told me. He would arrest outlaws, killers, and rustlers. It was up to property holders to settle their own arguments, gunplay or not.

Yet if Tharp could find nothing in me to dislike, it would at least help. My fighting must be in self-defense.

All the following day I worked around the place, cleaning up the debris left by the fire, and rebuilding the corral. but keeping a careful lookout. Some of the saddle stock had escaped when the corrals were pulled down. These I rounded up and herded back to the corral with my mules.

One young steer had suffered a broken leg in the drive on the Boxed M camp, so I shot it and butchered the caracass, hanging up the beef until I could jerk it.

I cleaned out the spring near where the house had stood, and built several rifle pits against possible attack. Then, mounting up, I ended my day by scouting the vicinity. No riders were in sight. All was still. The young stock were making themselves happily at home in the knee-high grass.

Three times I spotted good defense areas and mapped out routes that would offer cover in going from one to the other. Being a practical man, I also looked for an escape route.

I slept in a sheltered place near the spring and at daybreak I rolled out of my blankets and saddled up.

The morning was clear and cool. In an hour the sun would be warming the hills, but now a coat was a comfortable thing. Reluctantly, I put out my fire and swung into the saddle. The buckskin was frisky and tugged at the bit, ready to go.

Rounding a bend, I suddenly saw a dozen riders coming toward me at a canter. Wheeling the buckskin, I slapped the spurs into his flanks and went up the Wash at a dead run. A bullet whined past my ear as I swung into a branch canyon and raced to the top of the plateau.

Behind me the racing horses ran past the canyon's mouth. Then there was a shout as a rider saw me, and they turned back. By the time they entered the canyon mouth I was on top of the mesa.

It was the Pinders, and they were out for blood.

I dropped to the ground and took a running dive for a rock, landing behind it and swinging my Winchester to my shoulder at the same time. The butt settled, I took a long breath, then squeezed off my shot.

A horse stumbled, throwing his rider over his head, and my second shot nailed the rider before he could rise. Firing as rapidly as I could aim, I sent a dozen bullets screaming down the canyon. They scattered for shelter, a wild melee of lunging horses and men.

The man I'd shot began to crawl, dragging a broken leg. He was out of it, so I let him go.

Several horses had raced away, but two stood ground-hitched. On one of these was a big canteen. I emptied it with a shot. A foot showed and I triggered my Winchester. A bit of leather flew up and the foot was withdrawn.

Bullets ricocheted around me, but my position could not have been better. As long as I remained where I was they could neither advance nor retreat.

The sun was well up in the sky now, and the day promised to be hot. Where I lay there was a little shade from a rock overhang, and I had water on my saddle. They had neither. Digging out a little hollow in the sand, I settled down to be comfortable.

Several shots were fired, but they were not anxious to expose their position, and the shots were far off the mark.

Five . . . ten minutes passed. Then I saw a man trying to crawl back toward the canyon mouth.

I let him crawl. . . . When he was a good twenty yards from shelter I sighted down the barrel and put one into the sand right ahead of him. He sprang to his feet and ducked for shelter. I splattered rock fragments into his face with a ricochet and he made a running dive for shelter, with another bullet helping him along.

"Looks like a hot day!" I called.

My voice carried well in the rocky canyon, and somebody swore viciously. I sat back and rolled a smoke. Nobody moved down below.

The canyon mouth was like an oven. Heat waves danced in the sun, the rocks became blistering. The hours marched slowly by. From time to time some restless soul made a move, but a quick shot would always change his mind. I drank from my canteen and moved a little with the shade.

"How long you figure you can keep us here?" someone yelled.

"I've got plenty of water and two hundred rounds of ammunition!"

One of them swore again, and there were shouted

threats. Silence descended over the canyon. Knowing
they could get no water must have aggravated their
thirst. The sun swam in a coppery sea of heat, and
the horizon was lost in heat waves. Sweat trickled
down my face and down my body under the arms.
Where I lay there was not only shade but a slight
breeze, but where they lay the heat reflected off the
canyon walls and all wind was shut off.

Finally, letting go with a shot, I slid back out of
sight and got to my feet.

My horse cropped grass near some rocks, well under the shade. Shifting my rifle to my left hand, I slid
down the rocks, mopping my face with my right. Then
I stopped, my hand belt high.

Backed up against a rock near my horse was a man
whom I knew at once, although I had never seen him.
It was Rollie Pinder.

"You gave them boys hell."

"They asked for it."

As I spoke he smiled slowly and dropped his hand
for his gun.

His easy smile and casual voice were nicely calculated to throw me off guard, but my left hand held
the barrel of my rifle a few inches forward of the
trigger guard, the butt in front of me.

As his hand dropped I tilted the gun hard and the
stock struck my hip as my hand slapped the trigger
guard.

Rollie was fast and his gun came up smoking. His
slug struck me a split second after my finger
squeezed off its shot. It felt as if I had been kicked in
the side and I took a staggering step back, a rolling
rock under my foot throwing me out of line of his
second shot.

Then I fired again. I'd worked the lever unconsciously, and my aim was true.

Rollie fell back against the rocks. He was still
smiling that casual smile. Only now it seemed frozen

into his features. He started to bring his gun up and I heard the report. But I was firing . . . I shot three times as fast as I could work the lever.

Weaving on my feet, I stared down at his body. Great holes had been torn into him by the .44 slugs.

I scrambled back to my former position, and was only just in time. The men below, alerted by my shots, had made a break to get away. My head was spinning and my eyes refused to focus. If they started after me now, I was through.

The ground seemed to dip under me, but I raised my rifle and got off a shot, then another. One man went down and the others scrambled for cover.

My legs went out from under me and I sat down hard. My breath coming in ragged gasps, I ripped my shirt and plugged my wounds. I had to get away now. But even if the way were open, I could never climb to the cliff house.

Rifle dragging, I crawled and slid back to the buckskin. Twice I almost fainted from weakness. Pain gripped at my vitals, squeezing and knotting them. Then I got hold of the saddlehorn and pulled myself into the saddle. When I finally got my rifle into its scabbard I took some piggin strings and tied my hands to the saddlehorn, then across my thighs to hold me on.

The buckskin was already walking, as if sensing the need to be away. I pointed him into the wilderness of canyons.

"Go, boy. Keep goin'."

Sometime after that I fainted. . . . Twice during the long hours that followed I awakened to find the horse still walking westward. Each time I muttered to him, and he walked on into the darkness, finding his own way.

They would be coming after me. This remained in my mind. Wracked with pain, I had only the driving urge to get away. I pushed on, deeper and deeper into that lonely, trackless land made even stranger by the darkness.

Day was near when at last my eyes opened again. When I lifted my head the effort made it swim dizzily, but I stared around, seeing nothing familiar.

Buck had stopped beside a small spring in a canyon. There was plenty of grass, a few trees, and not far away the ruin of a rock house On the sand near the spring were the tracks of a mountain lion and of deer, but no sign of men, horses, or cattle. The canyon here was fifty yards wide, with walls that towered hundreds of feet into the sky.

Fumbling at the strings with swollen fingers, I untied my hands, then the strings that bound my thighs. Sliding to the ground, I fell. Buck snorted and stepped away, then returned to sniff curiously at me. He drew back from the smell of stale clothes and dried blood, and I lay staring up at him, a crumpled human thing, my body raw with pain and faint with weakness.

"It's all right, Buck." I whispered the words. "All right."

I lay very still, staring at the sky, watching the changing light. I wanted only to lie there, to make no effort . . . to die.

To die?

No. . . .

There had been a promise made. A promise to Moira, and a promise to a tired old man who had been killed.

Yet if I would live I must move. For they would not let me go now. They would hunt me down. Jim Pinder would want to kill the man who had shot his brother, and there was Bodie Miller, from Maclaren's.

Now . . . I must act now . . . fix my wounds, drink, find a place to hide, a place for a last stand. And it had to be close, for I could not go far.

Nothing within me told me I could do it. My body

was weak, and I seemed to have no will, but some-how, someway, I was going to try.

Rolling over, I got my hands under me. Then I started to crawl. . . .

SEVEN

PULLING MYSELF TO THE EDGE OF THE waterhole, I drank deep of the clear, cold water. The coolness seemed to creep all through the tissues of my body and I lay there, breathing heavily.

A sea of dull pain seemed to wash over me, yet I forced myself to think, to fight back the pain. I must bathe my wounds. That meant hot water, and hot water meant a fire.

Yet there was such weakness in me that I could scarcely close my hand. I had lost much blood, I had not eaten, and I had ridden far with the strength draining from my body.

With contempt I stared at my helpless hands, hating them for their weakness. And then I began to fight for strength in those fingers, willing them to be strong. My left hand reached out and pulled a stick to me. Then another.

Some scraped-up leaves, some fragments of dried manzanita . . . soon I would have a fire.

I was a creature fighting for survival, fighting the oldest battle known to man. Through waves of recurring delirium and weakness, I dragged myself to an aspen, where I peeled bark to make a pot in which to heat water.

Patiently, my eyes blinking heavily, my fingers puzzling out the form, I shaped the bark into a crude pot, and into it I poured water.

Almost crying with weakness, I got a fire started and watched the flames take hold. Then I put the bark vessel on top of two rocks and the flames rose around it. As long as the flames stayed below the water level the bark would not burn, for the water inside would absorb the heat. Trying to push more sticks into the fire, I blacked out again.

When next my eyes opened the water was boiling. Pulling myself up to a sitting position, I unbuckled my gun belt and let the guns fall to the ground beside me. Then carefully I opened my shirt and, soaking a piece of the cloth in the hot water, began to bathe my wounds.

The hot water felt good as I gingerly worked the cloth plugs free, but the sight of the wound in my side was frightening. It was red and inflamed, but the bullet had gone clear through and as near as I see, had touched nothing vital.

A second slug had gone through the fleshy part of my thigh, and after bathing that wound also, I lay still for a long time, regaining strength and soaking up the heat.

Near by was a patch of prickly pear. Crawling to it, I cut off a few big leaves and roasted them to get off the spines. Then I bound the pulp over the wounds. It was a method Indians used to fight inflammation, and I knew of no other than Indian remedies that would do me here.

It was a slow thing, this working to patch my wounds, and I realized there was little time left to me. My enemies would be working out my trail, and I had no idea how far my horse had come in the darkness, nor over what sort of ground. My trail might be plain as day, or it might be confusing.

There was a clump of amolillo near by and I dug up some roots, scraping them into boiling water. They foamed up when stirred and I drank some of the foamy liquid. Indians claimed bullet wounds healed better after a man drank amolillo water.

Then I made a meal of squaw cabbage and breadroot, lacking the strength to get my saddlebags. Sick with weakness, I crawled under the brush and slept, awakening to drink deep of the cold water, then to sleep again.

And through the red darkness of my tortured sleep men rode and fought and guns crashed. Men struggled in the shadows along the edge of my consciousness.

Morgan Park ... Pinder ... Rud Maclaren, and the sharply feral face of Bodie Miller.

The muzzling of my horse awakened me, and the cold light of a new day was beginning.

"All right, Buck," I whispered. "I'm awake. I'm alive."

And I was ... just barely.

My weakness frightened me. If they came upon me now they would not hesitate to kill me, nor could I fight them off.

Lying on my back I breathed heavily, trying to find some way out. I had no doubt they were coming, and that they could not be far behind.

They might have trouble with the trail, but they would figure that I was hurt and unconscious, that my horse was finding his own way. Then they would come fast.

High up the canyon wall there was a patch of green, perhaps a break in the rock. My eyes had been on it for some time before it began to register on my awareness. Sudden hope brought me struggling to my elbow. My eyes studied the break in the wall, if that was what it was. There was green there, foothold for a tree or two, and there seemed to be a ledge below.

Rolling over, I crawled along the ground to the waterhole and drank deep and long, then I filled my canteen. Now I had only to get into the saddle, but first, I tried to wipe out all the tracks I had left. I knew I could not get rid of all ... but there was a chance I could throw them off my trail.

Getting to my knees, I caught the buckskin's stirrup and pulled myself erect. Then I got a foot into the stirrup and swung into the saddle.

For an instant my head spun crazily as I clung to the saddlehorn. Then my brain seemed to clear and lifted my heavy head, slowly walking the horse forward. There was a trail, very narrow, littered at places with talus from above, but a trail. Kneeing the horse into it, I urged him forward. Mountain-bred, he started up, blowing a little, and stepping gingerly.

Several minutes passed and I clung to the pommel, unable to lift my head, needing all my strength to maintain my feeble hold. Then suddenly we rounded a boulder and stood in a high, hanging valley.

A great crack in the rock of the mesa, caused by some ancient earth-shock, it was flat-floored and high-walled, but the grass was rich and green. I could hear water running somewhere back in the rock.

The area of the place was not over seven or eight acres, and there was another opening on the far side, partly covered by a slide of rock. What I had found was a tiny oasis in the desert, but I was not the first to use this hideaway. An instant later I realized that.

Before me, almost concealed by the cliff against which it stood, was a massive stone tower. Square, it was almost sixty feet tall, and blackened by age and fire.

The prehistoric Indians who had built that tower knew a good thing when they found it, for here was water, forage, and fire wood. Moreover, the place was ideal for defense. Nobody could come up the trail had used, in the face of a determined defender.

Near the tower grew some stunted maize, long since gone native. Nowhere was there any evidence that a human foot had been here for centuries.

Riding close to the tower, I found the water. It fell from a crack in the rock into a small pool maybe ten feet across and half that deep.

Carefully, I lowered myself to the ground, then I loosened the cinch and let the saddle fall from the buckskin's back. When I had the bridle off I crawled to a place on the grass and stretched out.

There was still much to do, but my efforts had left me exhausted. Nevertheless, as I lay there I found myself filled with a fierce determination to live, to fight back, to win. I was no animal to be hunted and killed, nor was I to be driven from what was rightfully mine.

Regardless of what my enemies might do now, I must rest and regain my strength. Let them have the victory for the present.

There was food in my saddlebags—jerked beef, a little dried fruit, some hardtack. There was maize here that I could crush to meal to make a kind of pinole. There was squaw cabbage and breadroot. There were some piñons . . . and I saw signs left by deer and rabbits.

The deer droppings were shiny . . . evidence of their freshness. Deer still came here then . . . and I had already seen some of the blue quail that are native to desert country. So I would live, I would survive, I would win.

Near the wall of the ruined tower I made my bed. Working carefully, I erected a crude parapet of stones from which I could cover the trail up which I had come. Near it I placed my rifle and ammunition. At my back would be the spring.

Only then did I rest.

Slowly a week drifted by. I slept, awakened, cooked, ate, and slept again. Slowly the soreness left my wounds and my strength began to come back. Yet I was still far from recovered. Several times I snared rabbits, and once I shot a deer. Nobody came near, and if they came to the waterhole below I did not hear them.

When I was able to walk a few halting steps, I

explored my hideaway. While walking through the trees at the far end, I killed a sage hen and made a thick broth, using wild onions, breadroot, and the bulbs of the sego lily.

Several times I found arrowheads. They were entirely unlike any I had seen before, longer in design and fluted along the sides.

But a devil of impatience was riding me. The longer I remained away, the more firmly my enemies would be entrenched. Despite that, I forced myself to wait. The venison lasted, and I killed quail and another sage hen. I ate well, but grew increasingly restless. Several times I managed to climb to the top of the mesa and lay there in the sun watching the canyon up which Buck must have come during the long hours when I had been in the saddle.

The mesa that was my lookout towered above the surrounding country, and below me lay mile upon mile of serrated ridges and broken land. It was a fantastic land of pale pink, salmon, and deep red, touched here and there by cloud shadows. It was raw and magnificent.

But impatience was on me, and the time had come to move. My jerked beef and venison were long since gone. The quail and sage hens had grown cautious.

On the morning of the sixteenth day I saddled my horse. It was time to return.

Reluctantly as I left my haven, I was eager to be back. The deep, slow anger that had been burning in me had settled to resolution. Carefully, I worked my way down the trail.

At the waterhole I looked around. There were the tracks of two horses here. They had come this far, given up, and gone back. My trail then, was lost. Knowing nothing of my position, I followed the trail of those searchers as the best way to get back to the Two-Bar.

Before I had ridden three miles down the canyon I

began to see how difficult my trail must have been. I knew then that the two riders who had been at the waterhole had come there more by chance than by intention.

The canyon narrowed where a stream flowed into it, and following down the canyon the only trail lay in the bed of the stream itself. On both sides the walls lifted sheer. At places great overhangs of rock sheltered the stream and I splashed along in semi-twilight. Here and there the canyon narrowed to less than thirty feet, the entire floor covered by water.

Threading the boxlike gorges I came suddenly into a vast amphitheater surrounded by towering rock walls. Drawing up, I looked across the amphitheater toward a valley all of half a mile wide. Buck's head came up and his nostrils fluttered. I spoke to him and he remained still, watching.

Coming toward me, still too far to identify, was a lone rider.

EIGHT

REINING THE BUCKSKIN OVER INTO THE trees, I drew up and waited. Had I been seen? If so, would the rider come on?

The rider came on . . . studying the ground, searching for tracks. I waited, slipping the rawhide throng from my gun and loosening it in the holster.

The day was warm and the sky clear. The rider was closer now and I could make out the colors in the clothing, the color of the horse, the— It was Moira Maclaren!

Riding out from the shadows I waited for her to see me, and she did, almost at once.

My shirt had been torn by a bullet and by my own hands, my face was covered with a two weeks' beard and my cheeks were drawn and hollow, yet the look of surprised relief on her face was good to see.

"Matt?" She was incredulous. "You're alive?"

My buckskin walked close to her horse. "Did you think I would die before you had those sons I promised?"

"Don't joke."

"I'm not joking."

Her eyes searched mine and she flushed a little, then quickly changed the subject.

"You must go away. If you come back now they'll kill you."

"I'll not run. I'm going back."

"But you mustn't! They believe you're dead. Let them think so. Go away now, go while you can.- They've looked and looked, but they couldn't find you. Jim Pinder has sworn that if you're alive he'll kill you on sight, and Bodie Miller hates you."

"I'll be riding back."

She seemed to give up then, and I don't believe she really had thought I would run. And I was glad she knew me so well.

"Jim Pinder has the Two-Bar."

"Then he can move."

She noticed my full canteen, then waved her hand at the valley where we sat our horses.

"Father will be amazed when he learns there is water back here, and grass. Nobody believed anyone could live in this wilderness. I think you found the only place where there was either water or grass."

"Don't give me the credit. My horse found it."

"You've had a bad time?"

"It wasn't good." I glanced back the way she came. "You weren't trailed?"

"No . . . I made sure."

"You've looked for me before this?"

She nodded. "Yes, Matt. I was afraid you'd be dying out here alone. I couldn't stand that."

"Rollie was good. He was very good."

"Then it was you who killed him?"

"Who else?"

"Canaval and Bodie found him. Canaval was sure it was you, but some of the others thought it was the Benaras boys."

"They've done no fighting for me."

We sat there silent for a while, doing our thinking. What it was she thought I'd no idea, but I was thinking of her and what a woman she was. Now that I looked at her well, I could see she was thinner, and her cheeks looked drawn. It seemed strange to think that a woman could worry about me. It had been a long time since anyone had.

"Seems miles from anywhere, doesn't it?"

She looked around, her eyes searching mine. "I wish we didn't have to go back."

"But we do."

She hesitated a little and then said, "Matt, you've said you wanted me. I believe you do. If you don't go back, Matt, I'll go away with you. Now . . . anywhere you want to go."

So there it was . . . all any man could want. A girl so lovely that I never looked at her without surprise, and never without a quick feeling of wanting to take her in my arms. I loved her, this daughter of Maclaren.

"No," I said, "you know I must go back. Ball told me I was never to give it up, and I will not."

"But you can't! You're ill—and you've been hurt!"

"So . . . I have been hurt. But that's over and I'm mending fast. Sixteen days now I've rested, and it's more than time enough."

She turned her horse to ride back with me, and we walked a little in silence. "Tell your father to pull his cattle back," I said. "I want no trouble with him."

"He won't do it."

"He must."

"You forget, I'm my father's daughter."

"And my wife ... soon to be."

This time she did not deny it. But she did not accept it either.

At the edge of the badlands, after miles of argument and talk, I turned in my saddle.

"From here, I ride alone. It's too dangerous for you. But you can tell Morgan Park ..."

So I sat and watched her ride away toward the Boxed trail, thinking what a lucky man I'd be to have her.

She sat her saddle like a young queen, her back straight and her shoulders trim and lovely. She turned as if aware of my eyes, and she looked back, but she did not wave, nor did I.

Then I reined my horse around and started for town.

Often I shall live over that parting and that long ride down from the mountains. Often I will think of her and how she looked that day, for rarely do such days come to the life of any man. We had argued, yes, but it was a good argument and without harsh words.

And now before me lay my hours of trouble. There was only one way to do it. For another there might have been other ways, but not for me. My way was to ride in and take the bull by the horns, and that was what I meant to do. Not to the Two-Bar yet, but to town.

They must know that I was alive. They must know the facts of my fight and my survival.

I was no man to run, and it was here I had staked my claim and my future, and among these people I was to live. It was important that they understand.

So I would ride into town. If Jim Pinder was there, one or both of us would die.

If Bodie Miller was there, I would have to kill him or be killed myself.

Any of the riders of the Boxed M or CP might try to kill me. I was fair game for them now.

Yet my destiny lay before me and I was not a man to hesitate. Turning the buckskin into the trail, I rode on at an easy gait. There was plenty of time . . . I was in no hurry to kill or to be killed.

Rud Maclaren was not a bad man, of this I was convinced. Like many another, he thought first of his ranch, and he wanted it to be the best ranch possible. It was easy to see why he wanted the water of the Two-Bar—in his position I would have wanted it too.

But Maclaren had come to think that anything that made his ranch better also made everything better. He was, as are many self-made men, curiously self-centered. He stood at the corners of the world, and all that happened in it must be important to him.

He was a good man, but a man with power, and somewhere, back in those days when I had read many books, I'd read that power corrupts.

It was that power of his that I must face.

The trail was empty, the afternoon late. The buckskin was a fast walker and we covered ground. Smoke trailed into the sky from several chimneys. I heard an axe striking, a door slam.

Leaving the trail, I cut across the desert toward the outskirts of town, a scattering of shacks and adobes tha offered some concealment until I'd be quite close. close.

Behind an abandoned adobe I drew rein. Rolling a cigarette, I lit up and began to smoke.

I wanted a shave . . . sitting my saddle, I located the barber shop in my mind, and its relationship to other buildings. There was a chance I could get to it and into a chair without being seen.

Once I had my hair cut and had been shaved, I'd go to mother O'Hara's. I'd avoid the saloons where any Pinder or Maclaren riders might be, get a meal, and try to find a chance to talk to Key Chapin. I would also talk to Mrs. O'Hara.

Both were people of influence and would be valuable allies. I did not want their help, only their understanding.

Wiping my guns free of dust, I checked the loads. I was carrying six shells to each gun. I knocked the dust from my hat, brushed my chaps, and tried to rearrange my shirt to present a somewhat better appearance.

"All right, Buck," I said softly, "here we go!"

We walked around the corner and past a yard where a young girl was feeding chickens, past a couple of tied horses, and then to the back of the barber shop. There was an abandoned stable there, and swinging down, I led the buckskin inside and tied him.

It was a long, low-roofed building, covered with ancient thatch. There was a little hay there, and I forked some into the manger, then stood the fork against the wall and settled my hat lower on my head.

My hands were sweating and my mouth tasted dry. I told myself I was a fool—and then stepped out into the open. There was no one in sight.

Walking slowly so as not to attract attention, I crossed toward the back door of the barber shop.

The grass of the backyard was parched and dry, the slivery and gray old steps were broken and creaked as I mounted them. I looked through the glass in the door and saw that the only man in the shop was the barber himself. Opening the door, I stepped in.

He glanced up, then got to his feet without interest and went behind the chair.

"Haircut an' shave," I told him, "I been out prospectin'."

"Cowhand?"

"Yeah . . . an' I'll be glad to get back to it."

He chuckled and went to work. "Missed all the fun," he said. "Been lively around."

"Yeah?"

Rollie Pinder was killed . . . never figured the man lived was fast enough. Some folks say it was the Benaras boys, but they use rifles. I figure it was that there Brennan feller."

He snipped away steadily. Then he said, "We'll never know, prob'ly. Dead now."

"Brennan?"

"Uh-huh . . . folks say Rollie got some lead into him, seems like. They found blood sign."

The chair was comfortable. I closed my eyes. It would be good to sleep, to rest. It had been a long time since I had slept in a bed. With the quiet drone of the barber's voice, the comfort of the chair, I felt myself nodding.

"You'll have to sit up, mister. Can't cut your hair 'less you do."

So I sat up, but when he lay the chair back to shave me, my eyes closed again, and my body relaxed into the comfort of the chair. A hot towel on my face felt good. I listened to the razor stropping, slapping leather. Slapping leather, as I might soon be doing.

Smiling and half asleep, I felt the lather working into my beard under the barber's fingers. I was not quite asleep, not quiet awake. A rider went by in the street. The razor was sharp and it felt good on my face . . . I dozed. . . .

A hand shook my shoulder, shook it hard. My eyes opened into the anxious eyes of the barber.

"Look, mister, you better get out of here. Get out of town."

"You know me?" My face was free of the beard now.

"Seen you once . . . at Mother O'Hara's. You better go."

The little rest had left me groggy. I got out of the

chair and checked my guns. It was not a time to trust any man.

"Don't want me killed here, is that it? Don't want my blood on your floor?"

"That ain't it. I got nothing against you. Never knowed who you was until you got rid of that beard. No, you just move out. You ain't safe. That Pinder outfit . . ."

My fingers found the money in my pocket.

"Thanks," I said. "I enjoyed the shave."

Then I walked to the front door and looked down the street. Two men sat in front of the store. I put on my hat and lifting a hand to the barber, I stepped out.

It was only sixty feet to Mother O'Hara's, but it was going to be a long walk.

NINE

WALKING THAT SIXTY FEET, I KNEW A dozen men might be waiting to kill me. Unconsciously, I guess a little swagger got into me. It isn't every man who is hunted by a small army!

For an instant I paused by the window of Mother O'Hara's and glanced in. Key Chapin was there, and Morgan Park. I could not see who else. Down the street all was quiet. If anyone had identified me they made no move, and the barber had not left his shop.

My hand turned the knob and I stepped in, closing the door behind me.

The smell of coffee was in the air, and the pleasant room was quiet. Morgan Park looked up and our eyes held across the room.

"Next time you won't catch me with my hands down, Park."

Before he could reply I drew back a corner of the bench and sat down, keeping my guns free for my hands. The pot was on the table and I filled a cup.

"Chapin, an item for the press. Something like this: Matt Brennan of the Two-Bar was in town Friday afternoon. Matt is recovering from bullet wounds incurred during a minor dispute with Rollie Pinder, but is returning to the Two-Bar to take up where he left off."

"That will be news to Pinder."

"Tell him to expect me. I'll kill or see hung every man concerned in the killing of old man Ball."

"You know them?"

All eyes were on me now, and Mrs. O'Hara stood in the door of her kitchen.

"I know them ... all but one. When Ball was dying he named a man to me, only I'm not sure."

"Who?" Chapin was leaning forward.

"Morgan Park," I said.

The big man came to his feet with a lunge. His brown face was ugly. "That's a lie!"

"It's a dead man you're calling a liar, not me. Ball might have meant that one of your riders was present. One was ... a man named Lyell."

"It's a lie." Morgan Park was hoarse. He looked down at Chapin, who had not moved. "I had nothing to do with it."

This was the man who had struck me down without warning, who had held me helpless while he beat me brutally.

"If it's true," I told him, "I'll kill you after I whip you."

"Whip *me*?"

You could see the amazement in his eyes. He was a man shocked, not by my threat to kill, but by the idea that I, or any man, might whip him.

"Don't be impatient. Your time will come. Right now I need more time to get my strength back."

He sat down slowly and I picked up my cup. Chapin was watching us curiously, his eyes going from one to the other.

"Ever stop to think of something, Park?"

He looked at me, waiting.

"You hit me with your Sunday punch. Right on the chin. You didn't knock me out. You sat on me and held my arms down with your knees and beat me ... but you didn't knock me out."

He was staring at me, and if ever I saw hatred in a man's eyes, it was in his at that moment. This was the first time the story of his beating of me had come out. Many believed it had happened in a fair fight ... now they would know.

Also he was realizing that what I said was true. He had taken a full swing at my unprotected chin, and I had gone down, but not out. And he did not like the thought.

"Next time I'll be ready."

He got up abruptly and walked to the door. "Get out of here! Get out—or I'll kill you!"

On that he opened the door and went out, yet if he was worried, I was too. The man was huge. I'd not realized his great size before. His wrists and hands were enormous. Nor was that all. The man had brains. This was something to which I'd not given much thought, but he was shrewd and cunning. He was no hot-head. His beating of me had been a carefully calculated thing.

Mother O'Hara brought me food and Key Chapin sat quietly drinking his coffee. Others came in and sat down, stealing covert glances at me.

Rud Maclaren came in, and Canaval was with him. They hesitated then took seats opposite me.

The food tasted good, and I was hungry. Maclaren was irritated by my presence, but I kept quiet, not wanting to bait the man. He irritated me too, but there was Moira to think of.

Already I was thinking ahead. That amphitheater where Moira had met me . . . it would handle quite a number of cattle. It was naturally fenced by the cliffs, and had plenty of water, grass, and shade. And, while it was off the beaten track, it would be good to leave some cattle there to fatten up. With a good, tough old range bull to keep off the varmints.

Some of the men finished eating, and got up and left. I knew that out on the street they would be talking . . . about how I'd eaten at the same table with Maclaren and Canaval, how I'd told off Morgan Park— and that I was looking for the killers of old man Ball.

Canaval finished his meal and sat back, rolling a smoke.

"How was it with Rollie?"

So I told him and he listened, smoking thoughtfully. He would fill in the blank spaces, he would see what happened in his mind's eye.

"And now?"

"Back to the Two-Bar."

Maclaren's face mottled. He was a man easy to anger, I could see that.

"Get out . . . you've no right to that ranch. Get out and stay out."

"Sorry . . . I'm staying. Don't let a little power swell your head, Maclaren. You can't dictate to me. I'm staying . . . the Two-Bar is mine. I'll keep it.

"Furthermore, I'd rather not have trouble with you. You are the father of the girl I'm going to marry."

"I'll see you in hell first!" This was what he had said to me before.

I got to my feet and put a coin on the table to pay for my meal. The shave and haircut, the meal and the rest had made me feel better. But I was still weak, and I tired fast.

Katie O'Hara was watching me, and as I turned

toward the door she was smiling. It was good to see a friendly smile. Key Chapin had said nothing, just listened and waited.

Outside the door I looked carefully along the street. By now they would know I was in town. I saw no CP horses, but that meant nothing, so turning, I walked up the street, then went down the alley and to my horse.

There was a man waiting for me, sitting on the back steps of the barber shop. He had a face like an unhappy monkey and his head as bald as a bottle. He looked up at me.

"By the look of you, you'll be Matt Brennan."

His shoulders were as wide as those of Morgan Park himself, but he was inches shorter than I. He could not have been much over five feet tall, but he would weigh an easy two hundred pounds, and there was no fat on him. His neck was like a column of oak, his hands and wrists were massive.

"Katie O'Hara was tellin' me you were needin' a man at the Two-Bar. Now, I'm a handy sort. Gunsmith by trade, but a blacksmith, carpenter, holster, and a bit of anything you'll need."

"There's a fight on."

"The short end of a fight always appealed to me."

"Did Katie O'Hara send you?"

"She did that, and she'd be takin' it unkindly of me if I showed up without the job."

"You're Katie's man, then?"

His eyes twinkled. "I'm afraid there's no such. She's a broth of a woman, that Katie." He looked up at me. "Is it a job I have?"

"When I get the ranch back."

"Then let's be gettin' it back."

He led my horse and a mule from the stable. The mule was a zebra dun with a face full of sin and deviltry. He had a tow sack tied before the saddle, another behind. He got into the saddle and sat by while I mounted.

"My name is Brian Mulvaney, call me what you like."

Two gun butts showed above his boot tops. He touched them, grinning wisely.

"These are the Neal Bootleg pistol, altered to suit my taste. The caliber is .35, and they shoot like the glory of God."

"Now this," and he drew from his waistband a gun that needed only wheels to make it an admirable piece of artillery, "this was a Mills .75. Took me two months' work off and on, but I've converted her to a four-shot revolver. A fine gun."

All of seventeen inches long, it looked fit to break a man's wrist with recoil, but Mulvaney had the hands and wrists to handle it. Certainly, a man once blasted with such a cannon would never need a doctor.

Mulvaney was the sort of man to have on your side. I'd seen enough of men to know the quality of this one. He was a fighter ... and no fool. As we rode, he told me he was a wrestler, Cornish style.

It would be good to have a man at my side, and a man I could leave behind me on the ranch when we did get it back. How that would be managed I did not know, but somehow, it had to be done.

Yet there was a weariness on me. There had been little sleep or rest in the days since first I'd come to Hattan's Point, except during the sixteen days in the hills, and then I'd been recovering from a wound. And that wound had robbed me of strength I'd need in the days to come.

We scouted the Two-Bar as others had scouted it against me, and there were four horses in the corral. No brands were visible at this distance, and it did not matter. There was a log barricade that looked formidable, and obviously the men had been instructed to lay low and sit tight. They had seen us, and were waiting with their rifles. We saw the reflected light from a moving gun barrel, but we were out of range.

"It'll be a job."

Mulvaney put a hand on the sack in front of him. "What do you think I've got in the sack, laddie? I, who was a miner also?"

"Powder?"

"In sticks, no less. New-fangled, but good."

He rode his mule behind some rocks and as we got down he took the sticks from the sack. "Unless it makes your head ache to handle powder, lend me a hand. We'll cut these sticks in half."

We cut several, slid a cap into each stick, and tied it to a chunk of rock.

Darkness was near. It was time to move. We had waited under cover, but the men behind the barricade knew we were here, and by now they were wondering what we were doing. Perhaps they had seen the tow sacks, and were puzzling over what they contained.

Carefully, we gathered up our bombs and slid over the rim. We were still a good distance from the edge of the barricade. Suddenly, with a lunge, I was running. I had spotted cover just ahead, but a man sprang up from behind the barrier and he snapped a quick shot just as I slid into shelter behind the rock.

Mulvaney was running too. Another shot sounded, bu then I rolled up to my knees and hurled the first bomb.

I'd lit the fuse hurriedly and the flying dynamite charge left a trail of sparks. Somebody let go with a wild yell, and then the bomb hit and exploded almost in the same instant.

Mulvaney's first and my second followed, both of them in the air at once. Another explosion split the night apart and one man dove over the barricade and started running straight toward me. The others charged the corral. The man coming at me glimpsed me then and slid to a halt. He wheeled as if the devil was after him.

Four riders dashed from the corral and were gone.

Mulvaney got up from behind his rock and we walked to the corral. He was chuckling.

"They'd have stood until hell froze over for guns," he said, "but that giant powder got 'em."

Leaving Mulvaney, I returned for my horse and his mule. So again I was on the ranch. . . .

Standing there under the stars, I looked off toward town. They would go there first, or that was my guess. And that meant they would have a few drinks and it would be hours before another attack could be mounted. And Mulvaney had been right, of course. They would have fought it out with guns. The giant powder was frightening and different.

Walking back to the ranch yard, leading the horses, I met Mulvaney gathering wood.

"It's a fine ranch," he said thoughtfully, "and you're a lucky man."

"If I can hold it."

"We'll hold it," he said quietly.

TEN

We had eaten our noon meal on the following day when we saw a plume of dust. It seemed like one rider, at most not more than two.

Mulvaney got up unhurriedly and moved across to the log barricade and waited beside his rifle. He was not a man who grew greatly excited, and I liked him for that. Fighting is a cool-headed business.

Rolling a smoke, I watched that dust. It could mean anything or nothing.

No man likes to stand against odds, yet sometimes it

is the only way. No man likes to face a greater power than himself, and especially when there are always the coattail hangers who will render lip service to anyone who seems to be top dog.

It brings a bitterness to a man, and especially when he is right.

Yet this morning I'd no need for worry. The rider came into view, coming at an easy lope. And it was Moira Maclaren.

We had worked all that morning clearing ground for the new house I was to build. Moira drew up and her eyes went to the cleared space and the rocks we'd hauled on a stone boat for the foundation.

The house would stand on a hill with the long sweep of Cottonwood Wash before it, shaded by several huge cottonwoods and a sycamore or two.

"You must be careful. I think you had a visitor last night," she said.

"A visitor?"

"Morgan Park came over this way."

So he had been around, had he? And devilishly quiet or we would have heard him. It was a thing to be remembered, and Moira was right. We must be more careful.

"He's a puzzling man, Moira. Who is he?"

"He doesn't talk much about the past. I know he's been in Philadelphia and New York. And he takes trips to Salt Lake or San Francisco occasionally."

She swung down and looked around, seeing the barricade.

"Were the boys hurt?" I asked her.

"No . . . but they had a lot to say about you using dynamite." She looked up at me. "Would you have minded if you had hurt them?"

"Who wants to hurt anybody? All I wanted was to get them out of here. Only, that Pinder crowd . . . I'd not be fussy in their case."

We stood together near her horse, enjoying

the warm sun, and looking down the Wash over the green grass where the cattle fed.

"It's a nice view."

"You'll see it many times, from the house."

She looked around at me. "You really believe that, don't you?"

Before I could reply, she said thoughtfully, "You asked about Morgan Park. Be careful, Matt. I think he is utterly without scruples."

There was more to come, and I waited. There was something about Morgan Park that bothered me. He was a handsome man as well as a strong one, and a man who might well appeal to women, yet from her manner I was beginning to believe that Moira had sensed about him the same thing I had.

"There was a young man, Arnold D'Arcy, out here from the east," she said, "and I liked him. Knowing Morgan, I didn't mention him when Morgan was around. Then one night he commented on him, and suggested it would be better for all concerned if the young man did not come back."

She turned around and looked up at me. "Matt, when Morgan found out Arnold's name he was frightened."

"Frightened? *Morgan?*"

"Yes . . . and Arnold wasn't a big man, or by any means dangerous. But Morgan began to ask questions. What was D'Arcy doing here? Had he been asking questions about anybody? Or mentioned looking for anyone?"

It was a thing to think of. Why would a man like Morgan Park be frightened? Not of physical danger . . . the man obviously believed himself invulnerable. There must be something else.

"Did you tell D'Arcy about it?"

"No." There was a shadow of worry on her face. "Matt, I never saw him again."

I looked at her quickly. "You mean, he never came back?"

"Never. And he didn't write."

We walked down the Wash, talking of the ranch and of my plans. It was a quiet, pleasant hour, and a rare thing for me, who had known few quiet hours since coming to Hattan's Point, and who could expect few until this was settled and I was accepted as the owner of the Two-Bar, and a man to be reckoned with.

When she was mounting to leave, I asked her, "This D'Arcy—where was he from?"

"Virginia. He had served in the Army, and before coming out here he had been stationed in Washington."

Watching her ride away, my mind turned again to Morgan Park. He might have frightened D'Arcy away, but it was a matter to think about.

Behind Morgan's questions, and behind the disappearance of D'Arcy, there might be something sinister, something that Park did not want known. And yet he had been here during the night and hadn't killed me. Was it because he could not get a good shot? Or for another reason? Did he want me alive?

Mulvaney and I worked steadily around the place, but I rested from time to time, for my strength had not yet returned. We accomplished a lot, and by nightfall our foundation was finished and the shape of my house was plain to see.

Mulvaney was a steady and tireless worker. We each went to the rim of the Wash from time to time to look around the country, although the foundations of the house were almost as high as that rim now.

Toward evening, mounted on a gray horse, I scouted the country with care. I found tracks that must have been those of Morgan Park's horse, for they were the tracks of a big horse, the kind it would take to carry the weight of the man. I studied them, wanting to know them again. For in the back of my mind I had a plan shaping.

There were four sides to the question here at Hattan's. Jim Pinder and his CP, Maclaren and the Boxed M, myself on the Two-Bar, and Morgan Park.

Pinder could understand nothing but force. Maclaren, when he saw he could not win, would back off. He could be circumvented. But Morgan Park worried me.

It would be a good thing to learn something about Morgan Park.

There had been a Major Leo D'Arcy at Fort Concho, in Texas. A sharp, intelligent officer with a good bit of experience. The name was not too uncommon, but Major D'Arcy had, I believed, been from Virginia. He would not be a brother, unless a much older brother. He might be the father, or an uncle. And he might be no relative at all, but it was a chance, and I had to begin somewhere.

We cut hay for the horses that we had to keep in the corral, and by the time the moon was rising we were eating a leisurely supper.

"I'm going to Silver Reef tomorrow, Mulvaney. I'm sending a couple of messages."

"Have yourself a time. I'll be all right."

He looked down at the Wash in the moonlight. "It's a fine place this. I'd like to stay on."

"And why not? I'll be needing help."

I told Mulvaney about Morgan Park being near us in the night, and I could see he did not like it. We would have to be careful.

Rolled in my blankets I lay long awake, looking at the stars. The fire burned low . . . a coyote yammered at the moon, and somewhere a quail called inquiringly into the night.

Mulvaney turned and muttered in his sleep. And nothing moved along the western rim.

Into my mind came again the face of Morgan Park, square, brutal, and handsome. It was a strong face, a powerful face, but what lay behind it? What was there in the man? Who was he? Where had he come from? What was his stake here?

And what had become of Arnold D'Arcy?

Far off, the coyote called . . . slow smoke lifted from the embers, and my lids grew heavy. . . .

ELEVEN

SKIRTING WIDE, I HAD LEFT HATTAN'S Point to itself, and cutting through the broken land of bare rock and sand, I'd come to the trail to Silver Reef, and had seen no man during my riding.

It was very hot, and it was still. Jagged ridges thrust themselves from the earth, their crevasses and deep-furrowed sides filled with blown white sand. A dust devil danced before me and I pushed on, seeing the roofs of the town take shape.

There was no sound but that of my horse's hoofs on the hard-packed trail as I walked him down the last slope to Silver Reef.

The town lay sprawled haphazardly along the main street. There were the usual frontier saloons, stores, churches, and homes. The sign on the Elk Horn caught my attention, so I swung my horse into the shade in front of the saloon and dismounted.

"Rye?"

At my nod, the bartender served me. He was a bald-headed man with narrow eyes.

"How's things in the mines?"

"So-so. But you ain't no miner." His eyes took in my cowhand's clothing, and I knew he had seen my two tied-down guns when I came in.

"This here's a quiet town. We don't see many gun handlers around here. Place for them is over east."

"Hattan's?"

"Uh-huh. I hear both the Boxed M and the CP are hirin' fightin' men."

"Have one with me?"

"Don't drink. Seen too much of it."

My rye tasted good and I asked for another. That one I held in my fingers, stalling for time and information. It was cool inside the saloon, and I was in no hurry. My messages I would send in a few minutes. Meanwhile it was good to relax.

"Couple fellers from Hattan's in town the other day. Big man, one of them."

Inwardly, I poised, waiting. Somehow I knew what was coming.

"Biggest man I ever saw."

Morgan Park in Silver Reef. . . .

"Did he say anything about what was going on over at Hattan's?"

"Not to me. The feller with him was askin' after the Slade boys. They're gunmen, both of 'em."

"Sounds like trouble."

I tossed off my drink and refused another when he gestured with the bottle. "Not a drinking man myself. Maybe a couple when I come to town."

"Could be trouble over there at Hattan's." The bartender put his forearms on the bar. "That big feller, he went to see that shyster, Jake Booker."

"Lawyer?"

"An' a crook."

The bartender was not disposed to let me go so easily. The saloon was empty and he felt like talking. Pushing my hat back on my head, I rolled a smoke, and listened.

Morgan Park had visited Silver Reef several times, but had not come to the Elk Horn. He confined his visits to the office of Jake Booker or to the back room of a dive called The Sump. The only man who ever came with him was Lyell, and the latter occasionally came to the Elk Horn.

The bartender talked on, and I was a good listener.

He was no well of information, but the little he did know was to the point, and it helped to make a picture for me.

Morgan Park did not want to become known in Silver Reef. In fact, nobody knew his name. He had his drinks in the back room of The Sump, and if he was known to anyone aside from Booker, it was to The Sump's owner. He rarely arrived during the day, usually coming in before daylight or just after dark. His actions were certainly not those of a man on honest busines.

When I left the saloon I went to the stage station and got off my message to Leo D'Arcy. Then I took pains to locate The Sump and the office of Jake Booker.

Night came swiftly, and with darkness the miners came to town and crowded the streets and the saloons. They were a rough, jovial crowd, pushing and shoving but good-natured. Here and there during the early evening I saw big-hatted men from the range, but they were few.

Silver Reef was booming, and money was flowing as freely as the whiskey. Few of the men carried guns in sight, and probably the majority did not carry them at all. Several times I saw men watching me with interest, and it was always my guns that drew their attention.

One hard-faced young miner stopped in front of me. His eyes looked like trouble, and I wanted no action with anyone.

"What would you do without those guns?" he asked.

I grinned at him. "Well, friend, I've had to go without them a time or two. Sometimes I win . . . the last time I got my ears beat down."

He chuckled, his animosity gone. "Buy you a drink?"

"Let's go!"

He was urging a second one on me that I didn't

want, when a group of his friends came in. Carefully, I eased away from the bar as they moved up, and lost myself in the crowd. I went outside and started up the street.

Turning at Louder's store, I passed under a street lamp on the corner, and for an instant stood outlined in all its radiance. From the shadows, flame stabbed. There was a tug at my sleeve and then my own gun roared, and as the shot sped, I went after it.

A man lunged from the shadows near the store and ran, staggering, toward the alley behind it. Pistol ready, I ran after him.

He slipped and went to his knees, then came up and plunged on, half running, half falling. He brought up with a crash against the corral bars and then fell, rolling over. Apparently he had not even seen the corral fence.

He got his hands under him and tried to get up, then slipped back and lay still. His face showed in the glow of light from a window. It was Lyell.

His shirt front was bloody and his face had a shocked expression. He rolled his eyes at me and worked his lips as if to speak. He had been hit hard by my quick, scarcely aimed shot.

"Damn you ... I missed."

"And I didn't."

He stared at me, and I started to move away. "I'll get a doctor. I saw a sign up the street."

He grabbed my sleeve. "Don't go ... no use. An' I don't want to ... to die alone."

"You were in the gang that killed Ball."

"No!" He caught at my shirt. "No, I wasn't! He ... he was a good old man."

"Was Morgan Park there?"

He looked away from me. "Why should he be there? Wasn't ... his play."

He was breathing hoarsely. Out on the street I could hear voices of men in argument. They were trying to decide where the shots had come from. In a matter of minutes somebody would come down this alley.

"What's he seeing Booker for? What about Sam Slade?"

Footsteps crunched on the gravel. It was a lone man coming from the other direction and he carried a lantern.

"Get a doctor, will you? This man's hurt."

He put down the lantern and started to run. I took the light and began to uncover the wound.

"No use," Lyell insisted, "you got me." He looked at me, his eyes pleading for belief. "Never ambushed a man before."

I loosened his belt, eased the tightness of his clothing. He was breathing hoarsely and his eyes stared straight up into darkness.

"The Slades are going to get Canaval."

"And me?"

"Park wants you."

"What else does he want? Range?"

"No."

He breathed slowly, heavily, and with increasing difficulty. I could hear the boots coming, several men were approaching.

"He . . . he wants money."

The doctor came running up. In the excitement I backed away, and then turned and walked off into the darkness. If anybody would know about Park's plans it would be Booker, and I had an idea I could get into Booker's office.

Pausing in the darkness, I glanced back. There was a knot of men about Lyell now. I heard somebody call for quiet, and then they asked him who shot him. If he made any answer, I didn't hear it. Either he was too far gone to reply, or had no intention of telling. Standing there in the darkness, I studied the situation.

The trip had been valuable if only to send the

message, but I had also learned something of the plans that Morgan Park was developing.

But why . . . *why?*

He wanted to be rid of Canaval. That could only indicate that the Boxed M gunman stood between him and what he wanted.

That could mean that what he wanted was on the Boxed M. Was it Moira? Or was it more than Moira?

Park had seemed to be courting Moira with Maclaren's consent . . . so why kill Canaval?

Unless there was something else, something more that he wanted. If he married Moira, Maclaren would still have the ranch. But if Maclaren were dead . . .? Lyell had said, though, that what Morgan Park wanted was money.

Booker's office was on the second floor of a frame building reached by an outside stairway. Once up there, a man would be trapped if anyone mounted those stairs while he was in the office.

Standing back in the shadows, I looked up. I never liked tight corners or closed places . . . I was a wide open country man.

It was cooler now and the stars were out. There was no one in sight. Now was my chance, if there was one for me once I started up those stairs.

Up the street a music box was jangling and the town seemed wide awake. In a saloon not many doors away a quartet was singing, loudly if not tunefully, but in the streets there was no movement.

Booker had friends here and I had none. Going up those steps would be a risk, and I had no logical story. He was an attorney I had come to consult? But the lights in his office were out.

Yet, waiting in the shadows, I knew that I had to go up those stairs, that what I needed to know might be found there.

Glancing up the street, I saw no one. I crossed to

the foot of the steps and, taking a long breath, I went up swiftly, two at a time. The door was locked, but I knew something of locks, and soon had the door opened.

It was pitch dark inside and smelled of stale tobacco. Lighting my way with a stump of candle, I examined the tray on top of the desk, the top drawer, and the side drawers. Every sense alert for the slightest sound, I worked quickly and with precision. Suddenly, I stopped.

In my hand was an assayer's report. No name was on the report, no location was mentioned, but the ore that had been assayed was amazingly rich in silver. Placing it to one side and working swiftly through the papers, I came suddenly upon a familiar name.

The name was signed to a letter of one paragraph only . . . and the name was that of Morgan Park.

> *You have been recommended to me as a man of discretion who could turn over a piece of property for a quick profit, and who could handle the negotiations with a buyer. I am writing for an appointment and will be in Silver Reef on the 12th. It is essential that my visit as well as the nature of our business remain absolutely confidential.*

It was very little, yet a hint of something. The assayer's report I copied swiftly, and put the original back in the desk. The letter I folded and placed carefully in my pocket. Dousing the candle, I returned it to the shelf where I had found it.

The long ride had tired me more than I had realized, and now I suddenly knew what I needed most was rest. Before anything else, I must conserve my strengh. The wounds had left me weak, and although the good food, the fresh, clear air, and the rugged living were quickly bringing back my vitality, I still tired easily.

Turning toward the door, I heard a low mutter of voices and steps on the stair.

Swiftly I backed away and felt for the knob of a door I had seen that led to an inner room. Opening it, I stepped through and drew the door softly closed behind me. I was barely in time.

My hand reaching out in the darkness touched some rough boards stacked against the wall. The room had a faintly musty smell as of one long closed.

Voices sounded closer by and a door closed. Then a match scratched and a light showed briefly around the door. I heard a lamp chimney lifted and replaced.

"Probably some drunken brawl. You're too suspicious, Morgan."

"Lyell didn't drink that much."

"Forget him. ... If you were married to the girl it would simplify things. What's the matter, Brennan cutting in there, too?"

"Shut up!" Park's voice was ugly. "Say that again and I'll wring you out like a dirty towel, Booker. I mean it."

"You do your part, I'll do mine. The buyers have the money and they're ready. They won't wait forever."

There was silence, the faint squeak of a cork turning in a bottle, then the gurgle of a poured drink.

"It's not easy . . . he's never alone." It was Morgan Park's voice.

"You've got the Slades."

A chair scraped on the floor. A glass was put down, and then the door opened and both men went out. Listening, I heard their descending footsteps. From a window I saw them emerge into the light and separate, one going one way, one the other.

At any moment, Booker might decide to return. Swiftly opening the door, I went down the steps two at a time. When I came back to the street it was from another direction, and only after a careful checkup.

There was nothing more for me in Silver Reef. I must be getting home again. Only when I was in the saddle did I sort over what I had learned. And it was little enough.

Nobody knew who had killed Lyell, but Morgan Park was suspicious. Yet he had no reason for believing that I was even in the vicinity.

Lyell had denied his presence at the killing of Ball, which might or might not be the truth. Dying men do not always tell the truth, but his manner when questioned about Park's presence caused me to wonder.

Morgan Park and Booker had some sort of an agreement as to the sale of some property which Park could not yet deliver.

When he had said, "He's never alone" he could not have meant me. I was often alone.

It was not much to work with, and riding along through the night I told myself I must not jump to conclusions, but the man who was never alone could easily be Maclaren.

Or it might be someone else. It might be Key Chapin. Yet the remark about being married to the girl would not fit Chapin . . . or would it? Certainly, Maclaren's son-in-law would be a protected man in a well-nigh invulnerable position.

The more I thought of it, however, the more positive I became that the man must be Maclaren. That would be why the Slades were to kill Canaval.

When I was six miles from Silver Reef I turned off the trail into a narrow-mouth draw and rode back up some distance. There, under some mesquite bush, I made a dry camp.

It was after midnight . . . something stirred out in the brush.

This was lonely country, only desert lay to the north, and south the country stretched away, uninhabited, clear to the Canyon of the Colorado. It was a rugged country, split by great canyons, barred by pinnacled backbones of sandstone, a land where even the Indians rarely roamed.

In Silver Reef, I had stocked a few supplies, and over a tiny fire I fried bacon and a couple of eggs, then cut grass for Buck, and bedded down for the night.

In the moonlight the bare white stones of the draw bottom stood out clearly. The mesquite offered some concealment, and I was safe enough while the night lasted.

There was a tough sheriff in Silver Reef who might put two and two together if he talked to the bartender to whom I had talked.

When I awakened it was cold and gray in the earliest dawn-light. The clumps of brush were black against the gray desert . . . the sky was pale, with only a few stars. Over coffee I watched the stars fade out, then saddled up.

Buck moved out, eager to be on his way, and swinging wide of the trail I rode toward the ridge that followed the trail but lay half a mile away from it. Morgan Park would be riding that same trail. I did not want him to know I had been in Silver Reef.

There was no sound but that of the horse's hoofs and the creak of saddle leather. The black brush turned to green, the last stars faded, and the ridges stood out sharp and clear in the morning light. Great boulders lay scattered in the desert beyond the mountain's base, and here there were occasional stretches of sparse grass.

Once, looking toward the trail, I saw a faint plume of dust . . . a rider passing there.

Morgan Park?

It could be . . . and he might have seen my tracks.

TWELVE

SEVERAL TIMES I DREW UP, LOOKING OFF toward the trail. That lone plume of dust seemed to be keeping pace with me, yet I doubted if the rider was aware of my presence.

Where I rode there was little dust. We circled and climbed and dipped, and we had the rocky face of the mountain in back of us. Against that background I could not be outlined nor easily seen, but I held to low ground.

The wall of the mountain grew sheer, reaching high and straight up, its face without crack or crevice. At the base were heaps of talus, the scattered fragments of rock failling from the eroded sand stone. At noon I made camp at a small seep among a clump of trees. There was no sound . . . I picketed the buckskin on a patch of grass and rested, chewing on a chunk of jerked beef.

Resting by the water, I tried to plan. If Park was actually plotting some move against Maclaren, I should warn him, but he would not listen to me. Nor would Moira . . . she had known Morgan Park for some time, while I was a new and troublesome visitor. Such a story coming from me, and without proof, might do more harm than good.

Canaval . . . Canaval was the man.

He might not believe me, but he would be cautious, for he was a naturally cautious man and, like most gunmen, he trusted no one.

I must warn him of the Slades.

When I came back to Cottonwood Wash and the Two-Bar, the wind was whispering among the cottonwood leaves and stirring the tall grass. It was good to be home, and under me I felt the buckskin's gait quicken as he stepped into a trot despite his weariness.

Mulvaney stepped into sight as I rode past the boulder where I had waited on that day that now seemed so long ago, the day when I first saw old man Ball and waited for him to approach me.

"Any trouble?" I asked.

"No . . . some men came by, but the sound of my Spencer moved them along." He turned back to the cabin. "There's grub on the table."

Stripping the saddle from the buckskin, I looked around. Mulvaney had not let up on the work while I was gone, and what he had done was a day's work for two men. He was a good man, Mulvaney, and I owed a debt to Katie O'Hara for sending him to me.

"Trouble in Silver Reef?"

"A man killed."

"Be careful, lad. There's too many dying."

So as I curried the buckskin, I told the story, leaving nothing out, and Mulvaney listened, watching me. He was a good man and I had respect for his judgment.

"Right," he said, at last. "You'd best talk to Canaval."

Turning away from the corral I looked off down the length of Cottonwood, looked at the white-faced cattle grazing there, and at the water flowing through the ditch to irrigate the vegetable garden we'd planned. It was something begun. I was no longer dreaming. I was putting down roots.

Mulvaney had been watching me as we ate, sitting back from the fire and sheltered so no shot could reach us. "You're tired," he said. He had lighted his pipe, and he smoked quietly, then went on, "You'll back up that challenge to Morgan Park?"

"I will."

"He's a power of man, lad. I've seen him lift a barrel of whiskey to the length of his arms overhead."

He need not tell me that, me who had felt the weight of his fist. But how would Morgan Park be with a man who stood up to him? And one hard to hit? I was thinking that such big men rarely have to fight. Their size is an awesome thing and most men draw back. Had he fought much? Or had he always won easily and by bluff? I meant to see.

"Have you boxed any, Mulvaney? You told me you'd wrestled, Cornish style."

"What Irishman hasn't boxed? If it's a sparrin' mate you want, you've picked your man. It would be good to get the leather on me maulies again."

There followed a week at the Two-Bar that was uninterrupted, and it was a week of work, but a week of sparring, too. Only sometimes we went at it hot and heavy, and Mulvaney was a brawny man, a fierce slugger and powerful in the clinches. On the seventh day we did a full thirty minutes without a break; my strength was nearly back, and my side hurt hardly at all.

The rough and tumble part of it ... let Morgan choose the way. I'd grown up in wagon camps and cow camps. I knew my way around as a fighting man. After our tenth session with the gloves, Mulvaney stripped them from his hands.

"It's a power of muscle behind that wallop, lad! That last one came from nowhere, and I felt it to my toes!"

"Thanks ... I'll be riding to town tomorrow."

"To fight him?"

"To see Moira, to buy supplies, and to talk to Canaval. It is late for that. I've been worried."

On the day after my return two of the Benaras boys had stopped by on a rare trip to town, and I'd sent them to Canaval with a message from me—and to be given only to him. What might have happened since then, or what Canaval had thought of my message, I had no idea. And I was worried. Canaval could care for himself, but could Maclaren?

In my message to Canaval I had said there was some plot against Maclaren. I'd dared to say no more.

"And Morgan Park," I told Mulvaney, "I want the man mad. I want him mad and wild before we fight."

"It'll help . . . but be careful, lad."

Hattan's Point lay still under a noonday sun when my buckskin shambled down the street. When he'd been watered I walked into the saloon. It was not a drink I wanted so much as conversation. I wanted news.

Key Chapin was there, and as always, I wondered about the man. Where did he stand? What did he want?

"You've been making a name for yourself," Chapin said.

"All I want is a ranch."

"Lyell was killed . . . over in Silver Reef."

His eyes measured me, searching, but asking no question.

I shrugged. "You know there's a saying, 'If you live by the sword—' "

"They've got a sheriff who's serious about his business. They say he's asking questions."

Ignoring that, I asked one of my own.

"You said when I first came here that the town was taking sides. On which side are you?"

He hesitated, fiddling with his glass.

"That's harder to say since you came. I'm against the CP because they are essentially lawless men."

"And Maclaren?"

"Stubborn, and sure of himself. But at times he can be reasoned with. He has an exaggerated view of his own rightness."

"And Morgan Park?"

He glanced sharply at me, then looked out the door. He was frowning. "Morgan is generally believed to see things as Maclaren does . . . you don't believe that?"

"No . . . unless it so serves his interest. Morgan Park is anything to get the coon. He could choose any side if it would further his own interest."

At that, Chapin was silent, and I could see he was disturbed by what I had said, although for what reason I could not guess. He was Maclaren's friend, I believed, but he had also seemed friendly to Morgan Park.

"Look, Chapin," I said leaning toward him, "you're the press. I've seen a dozen frontier towns tougher than this one—and all of them were tamed. To get law and order meant a fight, but they got it. You more than anyone could lead such a fight here. And I'll help."

"Even to stopping this war?"

"What war? A peaceful old man had a ranch that two big outfits wanted. They tried to get it. They failed. He left that ranch to me. If protecting one's property is war, then settle down for a long fight."

"You could sell out."

"No. . . ." I took my hat from the table and was about to leave. "What you should do is start examining motives. How'd the fight start? Why not look into the background of some of the people around? And I don't mean Maclaren or Pinder."

"You haven't gotten over being sore at Morgan."

Standing up, I put on my hat. "Ever hear of a lawyer at Silver Reef named Booker?"

"He's an unmitigated scoundrel."

"Ask yourself why Morgan Park is meeting him in secret. And when you see the Slade Boys in town, ask yourself why they are here."

He looked up at me, definitely startled, and then I turned and walked outside.

Moira was not in town, so I turned the buckskin toward the Boxed M.

When I rode into the ranch yard the first person I saw was a cowhand with a bandaged foot. He started up, then realizing he was far from a gun, settled carefully back in place.

"Howdy . . . if you want to know, I'm visiting, not hunting trouble." I grinned at him. "I've no hard feelings."

"You've no hard feelin's? What about me? You darned near shot my foot off!"

"Next time keep your foot under cover. Anyway, why gripe? You haven't done a lick of work since you were hurt. Just sittin' around eating your head off!"

Somebody behind me chuckled and I turned in my saddle. It was Canaval.

"Did it for an excuse, Brennan."

"*Excuse?*" The injured man came to his one good foot, his face flushed. Then he saw we were grinning and, disgusted, he limped away.

Canaval turned to me. He took out his tobacco and began to build a cigarette.

"What do you want, Brennan?"

"Courting . . . you mind?"

"None of my business. Rud may not like it. He may have me order you off."

"If you tell me to go, Canaval, I'll go. Only one thing. If Park is here, you keep him off me. I'm not ready for him, and when I *am* ready I'd rather she didn't see it."

"Fair enough." His eyes twinkled a little and he looked up at me, only his eyes smiling. "You might be wrong about Moira. She might like to see it."

Swinging down, I loosened the girth a little and tied my horse to the corral. Canaval stood by, watching me.

"The Benaras boys were here."

"You got the message?"

He was alert and interested now. "Yes . . . I got it. Why would the Slades come here? Who would want to kill Rud Maclaren?"

"You figure it out . . . maybe somebody wants you dead so Rud will be alone."

He was not disbelieving me. I could see that, and I saw it with surprise. Did Canaval know something I did not? Or had something happened since my warning?

On the steps I stopped and looked back. "That same gent is saving me for dessert . . . and his own special attention."

He was standing there smoking when I knocked, and inside a voice answered that sent my blood pounding. It was a voice that would always have that effect on me, a voice that I would never hear too often.

As I entered there was an instant when my reflection was thrown upon a mirror beside hers. Seeing me gazing over her shoulder, she turned.

We stood there looking at ourselves. A tall, dark young man with wide shoulders in a dark blue shirt, a black silk handkerchief, black jeans, and tied down holsters with their walnut-stocked guns; and Moira in a sea-green gown, filmy and summery-looking, a girl with a lovely throat and shoulders, with soft lips.
. . .

"Matt! You shouldn't have come! Father will be—"

"He'll have to get over it sometime, and it might as well be now."

"That's foolish talk!"

She said it, but her eyes didn't seem to say it was foolish. Yet right at that minute, looking as lovely as she did, and surrounded everywhere by evidences of wealth and comfort, it may have sounded foolish even to me.

"You'd better start buying your trousseau. I won't have much money for a year or two, and—"

"Matt"—her eyes were anxious—"you'd better go I'm expecting Morgan."

I took her hands. "Don't worry, Moira. I promised

Canaval there'd be no trouble, and there will be none."

She was unconvinced and tried to argue, but I could only keep thinking how lovely she was. Poised, a little angry, her lovely throat bare, she was enough to set any man's pulse to pounding.

"Matt!" She was really angry, and a little frightened by the thought of Morgan Park coming. "You're not even listening! And *don't* look at me like that!"

"How else would a man look at a woman?"

She gave up then and we walked inside. The living room was comfortable, not in the ornate, overdecorated manner of the eastern cities, but with a simplicity bred by the frontier. Rud Maclaren was obviously a man who loved comfort, and he had a daughter who could shape a house to beauty even in this harsh land.

"Matt . . . how do you feel? Those wounds, I mean. Are you all right?"

"No . . . but much better."

We sat down, and for the first time she looked a little uncomfortable, and would not let her eyes meet mine.

"Where were you before you came here, Matt? Canaval said you were marshal of Mobeetie once."

"Only a short time." So I told her about that, and then somehow about the rest of it, about the long nights of riding, the trail herds, the buffalo, the border *cantinas*. About the days in Sonora when I rode for a Mexican hacienda, and about prospecting in Baja California, the ruins of the old missions, and much more.

And somehow we forgot where we were and I talked of the long wind in the vast ocean of prairie east of the Rockies, how the grass waved in long ripples. About the shrill yells of the Comanches attacking . . . and about nights under the stars lonely nights when I lay long awake, yearning into the darkness for someone to love, someone to whom I belonged and who belonged to me.

We were meeting then as a man and woman must always meet, when the world and time stand aside and there is only this, a meeting of minds and of pulsing blood, and a joining of hands in the quiet hours.

And then we heard hoofs in the yard, the coming of horses.

Two horses ... two riders.

THIRTEEN

Moira GOT UP QUICKLY, TENDRILS OF dark hair curled against her neck, and there were tiny beads of perspiration on her upper lip, for the day was very hot.

"Matt, that's father. You'd better go."

She had stepped toward me and I took her elbows and drew her to me. She started to draw away, but I took her chin and turned her face toward me. She was frightened and tried to draw back, but not very hard. Her eyes were suddenly wide and dark ... and then I kissed her.

For an instant we clung together, and then she pulled violently away from me. She stood like that, not saying anything, and then moved quickly to kiss me again. We were like that when we heard footsteps outside.

We stepped apart just as Rud Maclaren and Morgan Park came through the door.

Park saw us, and something in Moira's manner must have given him an idea of what had taken place. His face went dark with anger and he started toward me, his voice hoarse with fury.

"Get out! Get *out*, I say!"

My eyes went past him to Maclaren. "Is this your home, Maclaren, or his?"

"That'll do, Morgan!" Maclaren did not like my being there, but he liked Morgan Park's usurping of authority even less. "I'll order people from my own home."

Morgan Park's face was ugly. He wanted trouble, but before he could speak Canaval appeared in the door behind them.

"Boss, Brennan said he was just visitin', not huntin', trouble. He said he would go when I asked him and that he would make no trouble for Park.

Moira interrupted quickly. "Father, Mr. Brennan is my guest. When the time comes he will leave. Until then, I wish him to stay."

"I won't have him in my house!" Maclaren declared angrily. "Damn you, Brennan! You've got a gall to come here after shootin' my men, stealin' range that rightly belongs to me, and runnin' my cows out of Cottonwood!"

"We've no differences we can't settle peaceably," I told him quietly. "I never wanted trouble with you, and I think we can reach an agreement."

It took the fire out of him. He was still truculent, still ready to throw his weight around, but mollified. Right then I sensed the truth about Rud Maclaren. It was not land and property he wanted so much as to be known as the biggest man in the country. He simply knew of no way of winning respect and admiration other than through wealth and power.

Realizing that gave me the opening I wanted. Peace I had to have, but peace with Maclaren especially. And here it was, if I made the right moves.

"Today I had a talk with Chapin. This fighting can only be stopped through the leadership of the right man. I think you are that man, Maclaren."

He was listening, and he liked what he heard. He could see himself acting in the role of peacemaker. And he was a shrewd man who could not but realize that every day of this war was costing him men, cattle, and money. While his men were fighting or riding the country they could not attend to ranch business.

"You're the big man around here. If you make a move, the others will follow."

"Not the Pinders. You killed Rollie, and they'll not rest until you're dead. And he hates me and all I stand for."

Morgan Park was listening, suddenly hard and watchful. This was something he had never expected, that Maclaren and I would actually get together and talk peace. If we reached an agreement, any plans he had would be wasted, finished.

"If the CP try to continue the fight," I suggested, "they would outlaw themselves. In the eyes of everyone they would have no standing.

"Moreover, if this fight continues all the rustlers in the country will come in here to take advantage of the situation and steal cattle."

Moira was listening with some surprise and, I thought, with respect. My own instinct had always been toward fighting, yet I had always appreciated the futility of it. If we could settle our difficulties, the CP would be forced to restrain themselves. The joker in the deck was Morgan Park. If, as I now believed, he had reason to want to continue the fight in order to complete his plans, then an end to hostilities would be a death blow for his arrangements with Booker.

Rud was impressed, that was obvious to Morgan Park as well as to me. Maclaren rubbed his chin thoughtfully, seeing the logic of the situation as I expressed it.

Rud Maclaren was a careful man who had come early, worked hard, and planned well. It was only now in these later years that he had become acquisitive of power. But he could not help but realize that he was looked upon without affection by many of his neighbors. While he affected no interest, it was obvious that my suggestion offered an opportunity for that.

Park interrupted suddenly. "Don't trust this talk, Rud. Brennan makes it sound all right, but he has some trick in mind. What's he planning? What's he covering up?"

"Morgan!" Moira protested. "I'm surprised at you! Matt is sincere, and you know it."

"I know nothing of the kind. Yet you defend this— this killer."

He was staring right at me when he said it, as if daring me to object. That he wanted trouble, I knew. A fight now would ruin all I had been saying.

It came to me then, and I said it, not without doubt.

"At least, I've never killed a man who had no gun. A man who would have been helpless against me in any case."

When I said it I was looking right at him and something changed in his eyes, and into his face there came something I had not seen there before. And I knew now that I was marked for death. That Morgan Park would no longer wait.

It was D'Arcy I had in mind ... for, playing a hunch only, I believed D'Arcy had been murdered.

Yet it was more than a hunch. D'Arcy was a man who would never have neglected to thank his hostess. He would never have left without paying his respects. Something had happened to prevent it. But I had no evidence. Only that flimsy hunch, and the fact that D'Arcy had vanished suddenly after Morgan Park had shown an interest in him.

Now that I had started I did not intend to hold back. As best I could, I intended to put Rud Maclaren on his guard.

"It is not only rustlers," I said, "but those who have

other schemes as well, schemes they can only bring to success under the cover of this fighting."

Morgan Park's features were stiff. Actually, I knew little or nothing, yet somehow I had touched a nerve, and Morgan Park was a worried man. If my guess was correct, he now knew that I knew something and he would suspect me of knowing much more than I actually did.

"I'll think this over," Maclaren said finally. "This is no time to make a decision."

"Sure." I turned toward Moira and took her arm. "And now if you'll excuse us?"

We moved toward the door, and Morgan Park's fury suddenly snapped. His face livid, he started forward. Putting Moira quickly to one side, I was ready for him.

"*Hold it!*"

Canaval stepped between us, stopping Morgan Park in his tracks.

"That's all Park. We'll have no fighting here."

"What's the matter? Brennan need a nursemaid now?"

"No." Canaval was stiff. "Brennan promised me there would be no trouble. I'm not going to let you cause any."

There was a moment of silence, and Moira moved back to my side. What Morgan Park might have done or said, I do not know, but whatever it was, I was ready. Never before had I wanted to smash and destroy as I did when I faced that man. All I could remember was him sitting astride me, swinging those huge, methodical fists.

"Brennan," Maclaren spoke abruptly, "I've no reason to like you, but you talk straight from the shoulder and you are my daughter's guest. Remain as long as you like."

Later, I understood that right at that moment Park must have made his decision. There could be no other alternative for him. He drew back and slowly relaxed, and he did not say another word.

Moira walked with me to my horse, and she was worried. "He's a bad enemy, Matt. I'm sorry this happened."

"He was my enemy, anyway. That he is a bad enemy, I can guess. I believe another friend of yours found out about that."

She looked up quickly, real fear in her eyes. "I don't understand you."

"Did you ever have a note of acknowledgment from D'Arcy?"

"No . . . but what has that to do—"

"Strange, isn't it? I'd have thought a man of his sort would not neglect such an obvious courtesy."

There had been, I think, some similar thought in her mind. I had sensed it when I first mentioned that other friend. It was inexplicable that a man like D'Arcy should drop so suddenly from sight.

We stood there without talking, no more words between us for several minutes, but needing none. Our hearts were beating together, our blood pulsing together, our faces touched by the gentle hand of the same wind.

"This will pass," I said, "as the night will pass, and when it is gone, I shall take you back to Cottonwood Wash to live."

"You're a strange man. You look like an ordinary cowhand, but you talk like a man of education."

"I read a book once." I grinned at her. "A couple of them, in fact. And don't fool yourself about cowhands."

Tightening the cinch, I swung my horse for mounting.

"But could you settle down? Could you stay?"

My foot went into the stirrup and I swung into the leather.

"On the day I rode into Hattan's Point and saw you, I knew I would stay. Why does a man drift around?

Only because he is looking for something. For money, for a home, for a girl."

Night had closed in from the hills, moving its dark battalions of shadows under the trees and in the lee of buildings, then reaching out to cover the ranch yard. A few stars had come out.

Reaching down, I caught Moira's hand and swung her up, her foot slipping into the stirrup. Her breath caught as I pulled her into my arms, then came quickly and deeply, her lips parting slightly as she came into my arms. I felt her warm body melt against mine and her lips were seeking, urgent, passionate. My fingers went to her hair, and all the waiting, all the fighting, all our troubles dissolved into nothingness.

She pulled back suddenly, frightened and excited, her breasts rising and falling as she fought for control.

"This isn't good, Matt! We're too—too violent. We've got to be more calm."

I laughed then, full of the zest of living and loving and holding the beauty of her in my arms in the early night.

"You're not exactly a calm person."

"I?" She seemed to hesitate. "Well, all right, then. Neither of us is calm."

"Need we be?"

And then we heard someone coming down from the house, someone whistling lightly. Boots grated of the gravel path and I let Moira down to the ground quickly.

It was Canaval.

"Better ride . . . Morgan Park will be leaving soon. Might be trouble."

I gathered the reins. "I'm practically gone."

"Mean what you said back there? About peace and all?"

"What can we gain by fighting?"

Canaval turned to Moira. "Let me talk to Brennan

alone, will you? There's something he should know."

When she had gone back to the house, Canaval said quietly, "She reminds me of her mother."

Surprised, I looked down at him. "You knew her mother?"

"She was my sister."

"But ... does Moira know?"

"Rud and I used to ride together. I was too fast with a gun and killed a man with too many relatives so I left the country we came from Rud married my sister after I left, and from time to time we kept in touch. Then Rud needed help against rustlers, and sent for me. He persuaded me to stay." He hesitated, then added, "Moira doesn't know."

We were silent, listening to the night, as men of our kind would. I knew then that Canaval liked me or he would never have told me this.

FOURTEEN

IT WAS AFTER MIDNIGHT WHEN FINALLY I rode away from the Boxed M, leaving the main trail and cutting across country to the head of Gypsum Canyon.

Before leaving I had told Canaval what I had heard about the Slades, and he had listened, without comment. Whether he believed me I could not say, but at least he had been warned. Each of us knew all there was to know about Slade. The man was a killer for hire, a cold-blooded and efficient man with a gun.

There is a magic about the desert at night. Until you have seen it, stood alone in the midst of it, you cannot know what enchantment is. There is a stillness there and a nearness of stars such as no other place on earth offers.

I rode quietly and steadily, not hurrying, but feeling the coolness of the night, and remembering the girl I had left behind me, remembering Moira.

Mulvaney was waiting for me. "Knew the horse's walk." He nodded toward the hills. "Too quiet out there."

We turned in then, and rested, but during the night I awakened with the sound of a shot ringing in my ears. Mulvaney was sleeping soundly so I did not disturb him, nor was I even sure that I had heard it. A real shot? Or something in a dream? All was quiet, and after listening for a while I crawled back into the warmth of my blankets, of no mind to go exploring in the middle of a chill desert night.

In the morning I mentioned it to Mulvaney.

"Did you get up?"

"Yes, but I didn't hear anything. It might have been one of the Benaras boys. Sometimes they hunt at night."

Two hours later I knew better. Maverick Spring lay in that no man's land where the Boxed M bordered the Two-Bar, and I had ridden that way, for there was bog on one side of the spring and twice I'd had to pull steers out of there.

The morning was fresh and clear as I was coming up out of the wash. Heading across for the spring, I saw a riderless horse.

He was standing his head down and, suddenly worried, I picked my horse up to a canter.

Drawing near, I saw that a dark bundle lay on the ground near the horse. The dark bundle was a man, and he was dead. Even before I turned the body over, I knew it was Rud Maclaren.

He had been shot twice from behind, both times in the head.

He was sprawled on his face, one knee drawn up,

both hands lying in sight, on the sand. His belt gun was tied down. Rud Maclaren had been shot down from behind without an instant of warning.

After that one quick look, I stepped back and, drawing my rifle from the scabbard, I fire three quick shots as a signal to Mulvaney.

When he saw Maclaren his face went three shades whiter.

"This is trouble, lad. The country respected him. A man will hang for this."

"Feel of him, Mulvaney. The man's cold. It must have been that shot I heard last night."

Mulvaney nodded. "You'd best rig a story, Matt." It was the first time he had ever called me by name. "This will blow the lid off."

Of that there was no doubt, and I needed no argument to convince me that I was the logical suspect.

"No rigging. I'll tell the truth."

"They'll hang you. He's on your place, and the two of you had been feuding."

Standing over the body with Mulvaney's words ringing in my ears, I could see with clarity the situation I faced. Yet why had Maclaren come here? What was he doing on my ranch in the middle of the night? And who could have been riding with him?

Somebody wanted Maclaren dead badly enough to shoot him in the back, and had lured him here on some pretext. He certainly was not a man given to midnight rides. It had been late when I left his ranch and at that time he had been there. But so had Morgan Park.

The morning was cool, with a hint of rain. Mulvaney started for the Boxed M to report the killing to Canaval. It would be up to Canaval to break the news to Moira. And I did not want to think of that.

My luck broke, in one sense, Jolly Benaras came riding up the Wash, and I sent him off to town to report the shooting to the sheriff and to Key Chapin.

When they had gone, I mounted my horse and, careful to obscure no tracks, scouted the area. There was a confusion of hoof prints where his horse had moved about during the night, and at that point the sand was soft and there was no definition to any of the tracks.

One thing puzzled me. I had heard only one shot, yet there were two bullet holes. Crouching beside the body, I studied the setup. Strangely enough, only one bullet hole showed evidences of bleeding.

There were no other tracks that I could identify. They were mingled and overlapped each other, and all were indefinite because of the soft sand.

When I saw riders approaching I walked back to the body. The nearest was Canaval, and beside him, Moira. The other three were Boxed M cowhands. One glance at their faces and I knew there was no doubt in their mind as to who had killed Rud Maclaren.

Canaval looked at me, his eyes cold, calculating, and shrewd. Moira threw herself from the horse and ran to the still form lying on the sand. She had not looked at me or acknowledged my presence.

"This looks like trouble, Canaval. I think I heard the shot."

"Shot?"

"Only one . . . and he's been shot twice."

Nobody said anything, but all kept their eyes on me. They were waiting for me to defend myself.

"When did he leave the ranch?"

"No one knows, exactly." Canaval sat very still in the saddle, and I knew he was trying to make up his mind about me. "He turned in after you left—it must have been around two. Maybe later."

"The shot I heard was close to four o'clock."

The Boxed M riders had moved out, casually, almost accidentally it seemed, but shutting me off from any escape. Behind me was the spring, the bog, and a shoulder of rock. Before me, the riders formed a semicircle.

These were men who rode for the brand, men loyal, devoted, and utterly ruthless when aroused. The night before they had given me the benefit of the doubt, but now the evidence seemed to point at me.

"Who was with him when you last saw him?"

"He was alone. And if it's Morgan Park you're thinking of, forget it. He left right after you did."

Tom Fox, a lean, hard-bitten Boxed M rider, took his rope from his saddle.

"What we waitin' for, men? There's our man."

"Fox, from all I hear you're a good hand, so don't throw your loop over any quick conclusions I didn't kill Rud Maclaren, and had no reason to. We made peace talk last night and parted on good terms."

Fox looked over at Carnaval. "Is that right?"

"It is—but Rud changed his mind afterward."

"What?"

That I could not believe, yet Canaval would not lie to me. Rud Maclaren had been only half won over to my thinking, I knew. But that he could have changed his mind so fast I was not willing to believe.

"Anyway, how could I know that?"

"You couldn't," Canaval agreed, "unless he got out of bed and rode over to tell you. He's the sort that might do just that—I can think of no other reason why he would ride out durin' the night."

The one thing I had been telling myself was that I'd be in the clear because I had no motive. And here it was, the perfect motive. My mouth was dry and my hands felt cold . . . sweat broke out on my forehead.

Fox began to shake out a loop. I tried to catch Moira's eye, but she refused to look at me. Canaval seemed to be studying over something in his mind.

Nobody had drawn a gun, yet that loop in Fox's hand could snake over me quicker than I could throw a gun and fire. And if I moved toward a gun, Canaval would also. I didn't know whether I could beat Canaval or not . . . and he was a man I didn't want to kill.

Fox moved his horse a step forward, but Moira stopped him.

"No, Tom. Wait for the men from town. If he killed my father I want him to die, but we'll wait."

Reluctantly, Fox waited, and then we heard the horses coming. There were a dozen riders, with Key Chapin in the lead.

He threw me a quick, worried glance, then turned to Canaval. Briefly and to the point, the foreman of the Boxed M explained the situation.

Maclaren and I had talked, we had made a tentative peace agreement. Then Rud had changed his mind. Now he was dead, and I had been found with the body.

The evidence as he summed it up was damning. There was motive and opportunity for me, and for no other known person.

Looking at their faces, I felt a sinking in my stomach. You are right up against the wall, Matt Brennan, I told myself. You've come to the end, and you'll hang for another man's crime.

Mulvaney had not returned after informing the Boxed M of Maclaren's death. And there was no sign of Jolly Benaras.

"One thing," I said suddenly, "I'd like to call to your attention."

There were no friendly eyes in those that turned to me.

"Chapin," I said, "will you turn Maclaren over?"

He looked from me to the body, then swung down and walked over. In looking at Maclaren's face. I had lifted the body but had let it fall back in place. I heard Moira's breath catch as Chapin stooped to turn the dead man. He rolled him over, then straightened up.

He looked at me, puzzled. The others simply waited, seeing nothing, understanding nothing.

"You accuse me because he is here, on my ranch.
Well, he was not killed here. *There's no blood on the
ground!*"

Startled, their eyes turned to the sand upon which
Maclaren had been lying. The sand was ruffled, but
there was no blood.

"One wound bled badly and there must have been
quite a pool where he was lying because his shirt is
covered with it. The sand would be bloody if he was
killed here.

"What I am saying is that he was killed elsewhere,
then carried here and left."

"But why?" Chapin protested.

"You suspect me, don't you? What other reason
would there be?"

"Another thing," I added, "the shot that I heard
was fired into him after he was dead!"

"How d'you figure that?" Fox was studying me with
new eyes.

"A dead man does not bleed. Look at him! All the
blood came from one wound."

Suddenly, we were aware that more horsemen had
come up behind us. It was Mulvaney and the Benaras
boys, all of them.

"We'd be beholden," Jolly said, "if you'd all move
back. We're friends to Brennan and we don't believe
he done it. Now move back."

The Boxed M riders hesitated, not liking it, but
they had been taken from behind and there was little
chance to even make a fight of it if trouble started.

Carefully, the nearest riders eased back. The situation was now at a stalemate and I could talk. But it
was Moira I most wanted to convince, and how my
words were affecting her I had no idea. Her face was
shadowed with sadness, nothing more.

"There are other men who wanted Maclaren out of

the way. What had I to fear from him? I had already showed I could hold the ranch ... I wanted peace."

Then more horses came up the trail and I recognized the redhead with whom I'd had trouble before. With him was Bodie Miller.

FIFTEEN

BODIE MILLER PUSHED HIS HORSE INTO the inner circle, and I could see that the devil was riding him again. His narrow, feral features seemed even sharper today; his eyes showed almost white under the brim of his tipped down, narrow-brimmed hat.

Bodie had never shaved, and the white hair lay along his jaws mingled with a few darker ones. These last, at the corners of his mouth, lent a peculiarly vicious expression to his face.

He was an ugly young man, thin and narrow-shouldered, and the long, bony fingers seemed never still.

He looked up at me, disregarding the body of Maclaren as if it was not there. I could respect the feeling of Tom Fox, for his eagerness to destroy me was but a reflection of his feudal loyalty for Maclaren. There was none of that in Miller. He just wanted to kill.

"You, is it? I'll kill you, one day."

"Keep out of this, Bodie!" Canaval ordered, stepping his horse forward. "This isn't your play!"

Miller's hatred was naked in his eyes. In his arrogance he had never liked taking orders from Canaval, and that fact revealed itself now.

"Maclaren's dead," he said brutally. "Maybe you

won't be the boss any more. Maybe she'll want a *younger* man for boss!"

The leer that accompanied the words gave no doubt as to his meaning, and suddenly I wanted to kill, suddenly I was going to. In the next instant I would have made my move, but it was Canaval's cool, dispassionate voice that stopped me.

"That will be for Miss Moira to decide." He turned to her. "Do you wish me to continue as foreman?"

Moira Maclaren's head came up. Never had I been so proud of anyone.

"Naturally." Her voice was level and cold. "And your first job as my foreman will be to fire Bodie Miller."

Miller's face went livid with fury, his lips bared back from his big, uneven teeth, but before he could speak I interfered.

"Don't say it, Bodie. Don't say it."

So there I stood in the still, cool morning under the low gray clouds, with armed men around me in a circle, and I looked across the body of Rud Maclaren and stood ready to draw. Within me I knew that I must kill this man or be killed, and at that instant I did not want to wait for the decision. I wanted it now . . . here.

The malignancy of his expression was unbelievable. "You an' me are goin' to meet," he said, staring at me.

"When you're ready, Bodie."

Deliberately, I turned my back on him.

Standing beside the spring, I rolled a smoke and watched them load the body of Maclaren into the buckboard. Moira was avoiding me, and I made no move to go to her.

Chapin and Canaval had stood to one side talking in low voices, and now they turned and walked over to me.

"We don't think you're guilty, Brennan. But have you any ideas?"

"Only that he was killed elsewhere and carried here to throw suspicion on me. And I don't believe it was Pinder. He would not shoot Rud Maclaren in the back. Rud was no gunman, was he?"

"No . . . definitely no."

"And Jim Pinder is . . . so why shoot him in the back? The same thing goes for me."

"You think Park did it?"

Again I repeated the little I had learned from Lyell, and those few words in Booker's office.

The Slades were to kill Canaval—and why, except that Canaval was Maclaren's strong right hand? And it was Park who was hiring them.

This information they accepted, as I could see, with reservations. For Morgan Park had no motive that anyone could see. When I mentioned the assay report, they turned it off by saying simply that there was no mineral in this area, and there had been nothing to connect the report with Park. Nor did Morgan Park have anything to fear from Maclaren otherwise, for Maclaren had looked favorably upon Park's visits, had welcomed him, even treated him as a son-in-law to be. Maclaren had several times asked Moira, Canaval said, why she did not marry Park. All I had was suspicion and a few words from a dying man . . . no more.

Smoking my cigarette, I watched them start off with the buckboard. The Boxed M riders bunched around it, a silent guard of honor. Only then did I start toward Moira.

Whether she saw me coming, I did not know. Only she chose that moment to start her horse and ride quietly away, and I stayed behind, surrounded by my little guard, Mulvaney and the Benaras boys.

Bob Benaras had stayed behind to protect the ranch, and he was waiting for me when we rode into the yard.

"We'll be heading home," he said, "but Jonathan an'

Jolly, they can stay with you. I ain't got work enough to keep 'em out of mischief."

He was not fooling me in the least, but I needed the help, as he knew.

And then for a time, nothing happened.

With four men to work, the walls of the house mounted swiftly. All of us were strong, and Mulvaney was a builder. He was the shaper of the house, the planner of all our work. Forgetting everything, we worked steadily for two weeks. My side lost its stiffness and my muscles worked with their old-time smoothness. I felt better, and I was toughening up again.

There was an inquest over the body of Rud Maclaren, but no new evidence turned up. Despite the reports by the sheriff who rode out to investigate two days after the killing, many people still believed me guilty. To all appearances, there was not even another suspect. Jim Pinder had not even been in the county, and had a solid alibi, for on that night he had been in a minor shooting over a card game at Hite.

There had been no will, so the ranch went to Moira. Yet nothing was settled. Only, the Boxed M withdrew all claims upon the Two-Bar and any Two-Bar range or waterholes.

Jim Pinder remained on the CP and was not seen at Hattan's Point.

Of Bodie Miller we heard much. He killed a man at Hattan's in a saloon quarrel. Shot him down even before he could get a gun drawn. Bodie and Red were reported to be running with a lot of riffraff from Hite, many of them men from Robber's Roost. The Boxed M was missing cattle, and Bodie was reported to be laughing at the reports. He pistol-whipped a man in Silver Reef and was rapidly winning a name as a badman.

And during all this time I continued to think about

Moira. Once I rode over to the ranch, and Canaval met me in the yard. Moira would not see me.

Oddly enough, I thought there was real regret in Canaval's voice when he told me.

He was a quiet man, stern, yet not unfriendly. His hair was prematurely gray, and he had an easy way about him that drew friendships that he rarely developed. He was a lone wolf, never mingling with the men of the ranch, usually riding alone.

He said nothing about the Slades, nor did I ask him. I knew that he was closer to Moira than ever before. She relied on his judgment, although she knew more than a little of how to handle a cow ranch.

Maclaren had wanted more land. She began within two weeks after his death to make the most of what they had. For the first time in Boxed M history, hay was cut and stacked, and grain was planted for feed for the horses.

A fence without a gate was run along the line between the Boxed M and the Two-Bar.

The day they finished it, I was riding over that way. Tom Fox was in charge.

He rode out to meet me as I came near. His animosity had died, and we sat our horses, watching the fencing.

"No gate?" I asked.

"No . . . no gate."

She was shutting me out, cutting me off. Whatever might have been, had Rud Maclaren lived, his death seemed to have ended it, once and for all.

My thoughts returned to Morgan Park. He had gone back to his ranch and was not seen around, but he was never really out of my mind. There had been no sign of the Slades, and I could imagine what Canaval would be thinking.

There were changes with me, too. The old devil-may-care spirit was there, but it rarely came out. The work was hard and I kept at it steadily. My house was completed, and the garden we had planted was

showing signs of coming up. We had even trans-
planted several trees and moved them up to the
ranch yard.

We built furniture and we bricked up the waterhole. We planted vines around the house, and one
day we drove to town and loaded up household
things to carry back.

That was the day I saw Moira.

She had come from the post office in the stage
station and she was waiting for her buckboard which
was coming up the street from the general store.

She came out of the building into the sunlight just
as our wagon came by. I was behind, just putting my
foot in the stirrup, and looked over my saddle at her,
almost a block away.

I could not see her eyes, but as our wagon drew
abreast I saw her turn to look at the pots and pans, at
some rolled-up Indian rugs. Her face turned with the
wagon and she watched it out of sight, and then I
swung my leg over the saddle. As I turned the buckskin, she saw me and turned quickly away. Before I
could reach her she got into the buckboard and was
driving off.

It was a slow ride back to the Two-Bar, for wherever I looked I saw the pale, lovely features of Moira,
saw her standing alone before the stage station,
watching my wagon go by. These household things,
these might have been ours. I wondered if she thought
of that?

Jolly Benaras was waiting for me when I rode into
the yard.

"Nick was over. Said he seen tracks over east of
here. Three, four men."

Three or four men . . . in the broken, lonely country
to the east, the land where no man rode willingly.

"Where'd he see them?"

"Plateau above Dark Canyon . . . mighty wild country."

"Might be Bodie Miller."

"Might . . . he didn't think so. Bodie sticks close to towns. He likes to brag it around, playin' big-man."

Who then?

The Slades . . .

"Thanks," I said, "tomorrow I'll ride that way. I'll have a look. There's a valley over there where we could run some cows, anyway. I'll check it."

If it was the Slades, what were they waiting for? Had the killing of Rud Maclaren made it seem too risky to take a chance on more killings? It could be . . . and if anyone wanted what Maclaren had, Canaval still stood between them.

We moved the rugs into the house, put the pots and pans in the cupboards. I walked in the wide living room and looked around. It looked bare, cold. It was a house, but it was not yet a home.

At night I was restless. So much was left unfinished. Bodie Miller was around, rustling Boxed M cattle, no doubt. Sooner or later the Boxed M hands would meet him, and from talk I heard around, the least he could expect was a rope.

And there were the unknown riders east of us, lurking back in those mysterious, unknown canyons near the Sweet Alice Hills.

Saddling up a tough bay pony, I rode out toward the Maverick Spring where Rud Maclaren had fallen. In the darkness my horse made little sound as he cantered over the bunch grass levels.

We stopped at the spring and I drank, then watered my horse. It had been hours later than this when Maclaren was killed. . . . Suddenly my horse jerked up his head.

Instantly I was alert, and spoke softly to the bay. He had swelled his sides for a whinny but my low word stopped him. He looked off in the darkness toward the boxed M.

Moonlight silvered in faint strands, stretching away. The fence . . . Stepping into the saddle, my right hand resting on my thigh near my gun butt, I rode toward the fence, walking my horse from shadow to shadow.

Suddenly, I drew up.

There was a horse standing there in the darkness, a horse with his head toward me.

And in the night I heard a muffled sob . . . and my bay started walking again.

We were nearing the fence when the other horse whinnied. Instantly, a dark form sat erect in the saddle.

"Moira!"

An instant she sat stiff and still in the saddle, then with a low cry she wheeled her horse and spurred him into a run.

"Moira!"

Her horse ran on, but once I thought I caught the white flash of a face turned back.

"Moira, I love you!"

But there was no sound save the echo of my own voice and the pounding of hoofs, fading away.

For a long time I sat there beside that twin strand of wire, staring off into the night and the darkness, listening, hoping I'd hear those hoofs again, bringing her back.

But there was no sound . . . only a quail that called inquiringly into the night.

SIXTEEN

JOLLY BENARAS HUNKERED DOWN AND drew with his finger in the sand. His bony shoulders hunched against the morning chill, his right eye squinted against the tobacco smoke.

"Sure, that place you call the amphitheater, that's

here. Now right back of this here cliff is a trail. You can make it with a good mountain horse. When you get on top, that's the mesa above Dark Canyon. The trail I seen was over across, nigh six mile. There's a saddle rock over thataway, an' when you sight it, ride for it. On the north side you'll find that trail if the wind ain't blowed it away."

Jonathan had bunched forty head of cattle for me, and I walked to the buckskin and shoved my Winchester in the bucket. Then I stepped into the leather.

We started the cattle, but they had no mind to hit the trail. They had found a home in Cottonwood Wash and they aimed to stay, but we finally got them straightened out and pointed for the hills. Jonathan was riding along, but he would leave me when we got into the canyon.

He carried his Spencer in his hand, a lean, tall boy, narrow-hipped and a little stooped in the shoulders. His face looked slightly blue with the morning chill, and he rode without talking.

As for myself, I was not anxious to talk. My mind was not on my task. Herding the cattle up the canyon was no problem, for they could not get back past us, could only move forward. Nor was I thinking of the mission that lay ahead of me, the scouting of the group of men Nick Benaras had seen near Dark Canyon.

Had it really been Moira I'd seen? And if so, had she heard my call? Restlessly, I stepped up my pace. I was angry with myself and half angry with her. Why should she act this way? Did she really believe I'd kill her father? Both Canaval and Chapin had disclaimed any suspicion of me, although there were others who still believed me guilty.

Irritably, I watched the moving cattle, pushing them faster than was wise. Jonathan glanced back, but said nothing, moving right along with me.

At the amphitheater the cattle moved into the

grass, lifted their heads and looked around. We swung away from them and slowly they began to scatter out, already making themselves at home.

There was no sound but that of water running over stones. Jonathan put his rifle in the boot and hooked a leg around the saddlehorn. He rolled a smoke and glanced at me.

"Want company?"

"Thanks . . . no."

He touched a match to the cigarette. "I'll stay with the cows for a while, then. Maybe some of 'em will take a notion to head for home."

He swung his legs down and shoved his boot into the stirrup.

I was thinking of Moira.

"You take it easy, Matt. You're too much on the prod."

"Thanks . . . I'll do that."

He was right, of course. I was irritable, upset by Moira's action the night before, and I was in no mood for scouting. What I really wanted was a fight.

The trail that Jolly had told me about was there. Looking up, I backed off a little and looked again.

At this point the red sandstone cliff was all of seven hundred feet high. The trail was an eyebrow skirting the cliff face, and one which a spooky horse would never manage. But I was riding Buck, who was far from spooky, mountain-bred, and tough. He could have walked a tight wire, I think.

We started up, taking our time. It was nearing noon and the sun was hot. The cliff up which the trail mounted was in the mouth of a narrow canyon. The wall across from me was not fifty feet away, and as I mounted the distance grew less and less, until it was almost close enough for me to reach out and touch the opposite wall. I penetrated almost a thousand yards deeper into the canyon, then emerged suddenly on top.

Here the wind blew steadily. The terrain here was

flat as a floor, tufted with sparse grass, and in the distance a few dark junipers looking like upthrust blades from a forest of spears.

Sitting very still, I scanned the mesa top with extreme care. From now on I would be moving closer and closer to men who did not wish to be seen. No honest men would gather here, and if these were the Slades, then they were skilled manhunters, and dangerous men.

Nothing moved but the wind. Overhead the sky was wide and blue, with only a few tufts of lonely cloud.

I walked my horse forward, looking out for the saddle rock. In every direction the mesa stretched far, far away. I could smell sagebrush and cedar. Here and there on top of the mesa were tufts of desert five-spot, a rose-purple flower with flecks of bright red on the petals, and scattered clumps of rabbit bush.

My horse walked forward into the day. The air was clear and the chill was gone. . . . Suddenly ahead of me I saw the dark jut of the saddle rock, and closed the distance, keeping my eyes roving, wary of any rider, any movement.

At the saddle rock I dismounted to rest the buckskin, and let him crop some sparse grass. There was a niche in the black lava of the rock, and I led Buck back into it and out of sight.

Trailing the reins, I stretched out on the grass in the shade. It had been a long ride, and I had been late to bed and up early. After a few minutes, I dozed. Not asleep, nor yet awake. Several minutes must have passed, perhaps as much as half an hour, when suddenly I heard the sound of a trotting horse.

Instantly I was on my feet and, moving swiftly to Buck's side, I spoke softly. He eased down, waiting. The rider came nearer and nearer. I slid my Winchester from the scabbard and waited, holding it hiphigh.

Then I realized the rider would pass on the far side of the rocks, where Jolly had told me I'd find the trail. Swiftly, careful to make no noise, I climbed up among the jumbled rocks toward the saddle itself. When able to see the mesa beyond, I settled down and looked past a round rock.

For a minute, two minutes, I saw nothing. Then a horse came into view, now slowed to a walk. A horse ridden by a huge man, and there could be but one man of that size.

Morgan Park!

Where he rode I could see the dim tracks of other horses. After a moment of watching, I drew back and slid down off the rocks. Leading the buckskin, I walked around to where I could stand concealed, yet could see the trail ahead.

Morgan Park rode on until he turned, over a mile away, to the edge of the cliff. There he disappeared.

Waiting, for he might have stopped to watch his back trail, I let three, four, five minutes pass. Then I mounted and rode out to parallel the trail he had taken. The hoof prints of his big horse were plain, and I studied them. Also, the other prints that were several days old.

The day was hot. A film of heat daze obscured the horizon. Shimmering heat waves veiled the Sweet Alice Hills in the distance, the hills that seemed to end the visible world. From time to time the trail neared the lip of the mesa and I could look out over an infinity of canyons.

Yet when I reached the place where Park had disappeared, instead of the trail going over the edge of the mesa as I had expected, it merely dropped to a lower level and continued on.

Before me the mesa stretched ahead, apparently to the foot of the Sweet Alice Hills. But knowing that country, I knew half a dozen canyons might cut through the mesa before those hills were reached.

There was no sign of Morgan Park. He had vanished completely.

Riding on, I came to a fork in the trail. Here there was only flat rock, and, look as I might, I could find no indication of which way Park had gone.

Finally, taking a chance, I held to the trail that kept closest to the mesa's edge.

Suddenly the edge of the cliff broke sharply back into the mesa and showed a steep slide. From talks with the Benaras boys I knew this was Poison Canyon. So I went down the slide and ended in the bottom of a narrow canyon.

If I met a rider here, there would be nothing to do but shoot it out. No man could get back up that slide under fire, and one could only go along the canyon's bottom. I slid my rifle out of the boot and rode with it in my hand, ready to shoot.

The canyon bottom was sand littered with rocks of all sizes and shapes. The walls rose sheer on either side. There was little vegetation here, but many tumbled and dried roots washed down in the freshets that swept these canyons after rains.

Suddenly, I smelled smoke.

Drawing up, I listened, waiting, sniffing the air again. After a moment I got a second whiff of woodsmoke.

There was no cover here, so I walked my horse on a little further. A brush-choked canyon opened on my right, filled with manzanita. Swinging down, I led my horse back into it, pushing through the brush until I found an open spot with a little grass. I tied the buckskin to a bush and worked my way back, then slipped off my boots and continued on in my sock feet.

No air stirred in the canyon. It was hot, stifling hot. Sweat trickled down my body under my shirt. The hand that clutched the rifle grew sweaty. Careful to avoid thorns, I worked my way out through the manzanita and in among the rocks.

Here I hunched down behind a clump of mixed curl-leaf and desert apricot. Then, working forward on my knees, I crept deeper into the thicket.

The air was motionless ... the heat was heavy ... the leaves of the curl-leaf had a pleasant, pungent, tangy smell. I lay still, listening.

The smell of woodsmoke again . . . then a faint rattle of rocks, and the *chink* of a tin pan on rock.

Keeping inside the thicket of curl-leaf, I crawled forward. A lizard lay on a rock staring at me. His lower lids crept up, almost closing his eyes, his sides throbbed. My hand moved and he fled away over the sand. I crawled on, then waited, hearing a low mutter of voices.

Nearer, I could distinguish words. Settling down in the thickest part of the tangle of brush, with a rock in front of me, I listened.

"No use to shave. We won't get to Hattan's now."

"Him an' Slade are makin' medicine . . . we'll move."

"I don't like it."

"Nobody ast you. Slade, he'll decide." Tin rattled again. "Anyway, what you beefin' about? Slade will have the worst of it done before we move in. They's two, three men on the Two-Bar, that's all. 'Bout that on the Boxed M."

"Big feller looks man enough to do it himself."

"Then you an' me wouldn't have the money."

There was silence. Sweat trickled down my spine. My knee was cramped, but I did not dare to move. I could see nothing, for the curl-leaf thicket reached right to the edge of their camp.

I dried my hands on my shirt front, and took up the rifle again.

"Pinder'll raid today. Maybe that'll take care of it."

Pinder ... raid.

My place? Where else but my place? While I lay here in this thicket, Mulvaney and the Benaras boys might be fighting for their lives. I started, then relaxed. I could not get there in time now, and the Benaras boys were no chickens. Neither was Mulvaney. Their position was strong and they had food and water.

"Who gets Brennan?"

"How should I know? Big feller maybe."

"He's welcome."

"Finish that coffee. I want to wash up."

"You can't. Slade ain't et yet."

There was silence then. Cautiously I straightened my leg, then eased away from the rock. Carefully, I began to retreat through the thicket.

A branch hooked on my shirt, then whipped loose, a dry, rasping sound in the thicket.

"What was that?"

I held very still, holding my breath.

"Aw, you're too jumpy. Settle down."

"I heard somethin'."

"Coyote, maybe."

"In this close to us? You crazy?"

Footsteps sounded, and I eased my rifle into position, mentally retracing my steps to my horse. Where were Morgan Park and Slade? I might have to ride in a hurry and I knew no way out but up the slide, which would be impossible under gunfire.

"You goin' in there? If you do, you're crazy." The speaker chuckled. "You got too much imagination. An' if there was anybody in there, what would happen to you? He'd see you first."

The footsteps stopped . . . hesitated. A sound of brush against leather came to me, and I put my thumb on the hammer of the Winchester. I knew right where the man was standing and at this distance with a rifle I could not miss. Whatever happened afterward, that first man was as good as dead.

He didn't like it. I could almost see his mind working. He suddenly decided he had heard nothing.

He still stood there, and I gambled and eased back

a little further. There was no sound, and I withdrew stealthily to my horse.

Mounting, I walked the horse out of the brush-choked canyon and started back toward the slide. But when I reached it I went on past.

Around a bend I drew up and taking out a hand-kerchief, mopped my face.

Then I walked my horse deeper into the unknown canyon. I'd found what I wanted to know. Slade and his gang were here. They were waiting to strike. Even now they were meeting with Morgan Park.
. . .

Tomorrow?

SEVENTEEN

IT WAS MIDAFTERNOON BEFORE I FOUND a trail out of Poison Canyon. It was at the head of the canyon, and I came up out of it heading almost due east. Rounding the end of the canyon, I started back along Dark Canyon Plateau.

At sundown there still was far to go, and when my horse began to tug the bit toward the north, I let him have his head. Ten minutes later we had come up to a spring.

My horse was dead beat and so was I. It would soon be dark, and the trail was only vaguely familiar to me. The spring stood in a small grove of aspens over against the mountain. There were tracks of deer and wild horses, but no tracks of shod horses, nor of men.

Stripping the saddle from the buckskin, I gave him a hurried rubdown with a handful of dry grass, and picketed him out on a patch of grass. Impatient as I was, I knew better than to arrive home on a worn-out horse.

Behind me the Sweet Alice Hills lifted their rough shoulders, all of a thousand feet higher than the spring where I was camped. Eastward the sun was setting over the Blue Mountains and, hunkered down over a tiny fire, I prepared my supper, worried and on edge because of all that might be happening.

Yet, as the evening drew on, my anxiety left me. The hills were silent and dark. There was only a faint trickling of water from the spring, and the comfortable, quieting sound of my horse cropping grass.

Putting on more coffee I sat back, watching the fire, but far enough away from it to be out of sight. But I was not worried. I had strayed well away from the trail across the plateau, and if Morgan Park elected to return that night, there was no danger that he could find me.

Finally, banking my fire, I rolled in my blankets and was ready to sleep. But in those last minutes before I slept I decided what to do. Up to now we had been attacked; now I would stage a one-man counterattack. I would strike at the home ranch of the CP.

At daybreak, when long streamers of mist lay in the canyons, I was up and making coffee. As soon as I had eaten I saddled up and started back, and I rode swiftly.

The CP lay among low, rolling hills covered with sparse grass and salt-bush. Here and there were were clumps of snowberry. Along the slopes were scattered piñon and juniper, and weaving among them I worked my way close to the ranch.

It lay deserted and still. A windmill turned lazily, and there were a few horses in the corral. Watching, I saw a big-bellied, greasy cook come to the door and throw out a pan of water.

He stood on the steps, mopping his face with a

towel, then turned back inside. When the door closed, I swung to the saddle again, rode close, then suddenly spurred my horse and went into the yard on a dead run.

As I had planned, the sound of the racing horse brought the cook running to the door. He rushed outside and I slid my horse to a stop, with my gun on him.

His face went pale, then red. He started to speak but I dropped off my horse, turned him around, and tied him up. Then I grabbed him by the collar, dragged him inside, and rolled him under the bed. He promptly began to yell so I rolled him out and gagged him solidly.

Outside once more, I took down the corral bars and hazed all the fresh horses out and drove them off. Rummaging around in the tool shed, I found some giant powder that had been used to blast rock. I went back into the house and raised up a stone in the back wall of the fireplace and put the can of powder in the hole, then trailed a short fuse from it into the fireplace itself.

Finding several shotgun shells, I scattered them around and brushed ashes over them. Then I placed a few logs carefully over them, and filled a can with water for coffee and placed it on top.

Returning to the brush on a little bench overlooking the ranch, I settled down for a long wait.

A slow hour passed. The leaf mold upon which I lay was soft and comfortable. Several times I dozed a little, weary from my long ride. Once a rattler crawled by within a few feet of my head. A packrat stared at me, his nose twitching. He came closer and looked again. Crows quarreled in the trees above me.

. . .

And then I saw the riders. One look was enough.

Whatever had happened at the Two-Bar, these men were not victorious. There were nine in the group and two were bandaged, one with his skull bound up, the other with an arm in a sling. Another was being brought home tied over his saddle, head and heels hanging.

Lifting my rifle, I waited until they were down the hill and close to the house. Then I put my rifle to my shoulder and fired three times as fast as I could trigger the rifle.

A horse screamed and leaped into the air, half-turning and scattering the group. A man grabbed at his leg, lost balance and fell, his foot catching in the stirrup. His horse raced fifty yards, then stopped.

As one man they had scattered, some for the barn, others for the main house or the bunkhouse.

Two bullets I put into the barn wall, and then turned and shot at the hinges on the kitchen door. Two bullets in the lower hinge, then two in the upper. Taking time out, I reloaded.

The door hung in place, but I was sure the shots had gone true. Shifting my aim I smashed a window, holding the sight just above the sill where a head would be apt to be. Then I shifted and broke another window, swinging the rifle further to fire at an ambitious cowhand who was trying to get a shot at me from the barn door.

I took aim at the top hinge again, and taking up the slack of the trigger, eased back. The rifle leaped in my hands and the door sagged. Hastily I shifted my aim to the lower hinge and finished it off with two more shots.

My position was perfect. I lay among rocks and brush on a bench overlooking the ranch yard, where the barn door, the rear of the house and every inch of the space around the bunkhouse door were visible. Nor was there any way for a man to slip out and get into the brush without exposing himself. There was no cover away from the ranch buildings.

The door was open now, and I put two rifle bullets through the opening, heard a startled yelp from one of the men, then fired again, knocking more glass out of the window. Although I still had shells in the rifle, I took time out to refill the magazine.

Several minutes passed. I put the rifle down and rolled a smoke. Shifting my position to one more comfortable, I waited. A couple of tentative shots were fired from the house, both wide of my position.

One man suddenly ducked from the barn and darted toward a heavily planked water trough. I let him run, then as he dove behind the trough I put two bullets through it, right over his head, letting the water drain out over his head and shoulders. When he made a move, I put a bullet into the dirt beside him.

Waiting, I saw his rifle barrel come up. His position was a little better, but obviously he was trying to reach the corner of the corral from which he might outflank me. His rifle barrel was steadied against the post at the end of the trough. Taking careful aim at the edge of the post just above the rifle, I fired.

The rifle fell and the man slumped to the ground, whether dead or merely grazed, I could not tell. After that there was no more effort to escape from either barn or house.

The afternoon wore on. It was time I was moving, but I waited, wanting to see what would happen when they started a fire to make coffee.

Once I put a shot through the door to let them know I had not gone.

Crawling back to my saddlebags, I took a piece of jerked beef and my canteen from the saddle. Then I returned and settled into place again.

It was almost evening before a slow trail of smoke began to lift from the fireplace. Chuckling with anticipation, I waited. There was very little time left to me. Once it was dark I could not keep them under cover; and my position would speedily become untenable.

Now the smoke was lifting. Easing back to my saddle, I replaced the canteen and got my horse ready for a fast leave-taking. A shot through the barn door was enough to let them know I was still there.

The smoke increased, and suddenly there was an explosion within the house.

A shotgun shell . . . suddenly three others went, one, two, three! There were startled yells within the house and one man sprang for the door, but a bullet into the step nearly tore his toe off, and he ducked back into the house. Running back, I swung into the saddle, and almost at the same instant there was a heavy concussion and flame blasted out of the chimney. The chimney sagged, and smoke and fire burst from a hole at ground level.

It was enough for me. I swung the buckskin and took to the hills. Behind me there were shouts and yells, but they had not seen me. Then another crash . . . from the ridge I looked back, and saw that the chimney had fallen. There was a hole in the end of the house where the roof had been smashed in, and smoke was coming out.

Jim Pinder knew now it was no longer a battle in which he did all the striking . . . his opponent was striking back.

Avoiding the usual trails, I started for the Two-Bar. They would be worried about me, and they themselves might have suffered from the attack. But my day-long siege of the CP had given me satisfaction, if nothing more.

Mulvaney saw me coming and walked down to open the gate. A quick look showed me he was uninjured. The Benaras boys came out when I swung down from my horse and both of them were grinning.

Jonathan told me of the fight. The two boys had gone out from the ranch when they first spotted the approaching riders. Fighting as skirmishers, they had retreated steadly until in position to be covered by Mulvaney.

They had wounded one man and killed another before the attack even began. Then they fought it out from the bunkhouse, with all the weapons on the place loaded and at hand.

The CP had retreated, then tried a second time and been beaten off again. After that they listened and could hear an argument among the raiders. Pinder wanted another attack, but he was getting no support. Finally they had picked up the dead man and, mounting, they'd retreated down the wash.

We talked it over, discussing a new plan of defense. Then suddenly Jonathan turned around.

"Say! I been forgettin'. Bodie Miller shot Canaval!"

"Canaval? . . . "

"Took four bullets before he went down."

"Dead?"

"Not the last we heard."

"Miller?"

"Not a scratch."

Canaval . . . beaten by Bodie Miller.

Canaval had been a man with whom I could reason. He had a cool, dispassionate judgment, and dangerous as he undoubtedly was in any kind of a fight, he never made a wrong or hasty move. Moreover, with Canaval on hand there was always protection for Moira. And I had an idea that now she was going to need it.

Jonathan talked on. There was strong feeling against me in town, and it had grown since he was last in. Undoubtedly somebody was stirring it up. It was even said that Miller and I, despite our reported trouble, were working together, that I had instigated Miller's shooting of Canaval.

The firelight flickered on our faces . . . Jolly was out on guard, the night was still. It is a lonely business when one fights alone, or almost alone. It is not easy to stand against the feelings of a community.

Bodie Miller would not rest with this. Canaval had been a big name where men talked of gunfighters and gunmen, and now he was down and might be dying. Bodie's hatred of me would feed upon this triumph, it would fatten, and he would want a show-down.

There was little time. I must see Canaval if he was alive. I must talk to him. He must know of Slade and his gang, and what their presence implied.

Miller would not wait long to try to kill again. At any time we might meet, and win or lose, I might be out of the fight for weeks to come.

I would ride to the Boxed M. I would ride tonight.

EIGHTEEN

KEY CHAPIN WAS DISMOUNTING AT THE veranda of the ranch house when I rode into the yard at the Boxed M. He turned toward me, then stopped. Fox was walking across the yard and in his hands he held a Winchester.

"Get off the place, Brennan!"

"I've got business here."

"You get! You're covered from the bunkhouse an' the barn, so don't start for a gun."

"Don't ride me, Fox. I won't take it."

The buckskin started on toward the house and Fox stepped back, hesitated, then started to lift his rifle. Although I wasn't looking at him, I could sense that rifle coming up, and debated my chances, remembering those guns behind me.

"Fox!" It was Moira, her voice clear and cool. "Let the gentleman come up."

Slowly the rifle lowered, and for an instant I drew rein, "I'm glad she stopped you, Fox. You're too good a man to die."

The sincerity in my voice must have registered, for

he looked at me with a puzzled glance, then turned away toward the bunkhouse.

There was no welcome in Moira's eyes. Her face was cool, composed.

"Was there something you wanted?"

"Is that my only welcome?"

Her glaze did not flicker or change. "Had you reason to expect more?"

"No, Moira. I guess I didn't."

The lines around her mouth softened a little, but she merely waited, looking at me.

"How's Canaval?"

"Resting."

"Is he conscious?"

"Yes . . . but he will see no one."

From the window Canaval's voice carried to me. "Brennan, is that you? Come in, man!"

Moira hesitated, and for a minute I believed she would refuse to admit me. Then she stepped aside and I went in. She followed me, and Chapin came behind her.

Canaval's appearance shocked me. He was drawn and thin, his eyes huge against the ghastly pallor of his face. His hand gripped mine hard.

"Watch that little demon, Matt! He's fast! He had a bullet in me before my gun cleared. He's a freak! Nerves all wrapped up tight, then lets go like a tight-coiled spring."

He put a hand on my sleeve.

"Wanted to tell you. I found tracks not far from here. Tracks of a man carrying a heavy burden. Not your tracks. Big man . . . small feet."

We were all thinking the same thing then. I could see it in Moira's startled eyes. Morgan Park had small feet. Chapin let his breath out slowly.

"Brennan, I was going to ride over your way when I left here. A message for you. Picked up in Silver Reef yesterday."

It was a telegram, still sealed. I ripped it open and read:

MY BROTHER UNHEARD OF IN MANY MONTHS. MORGAN PARK ANSWERS DESCRIPTION OF PARK CANTWELL, WANTED FOR MURDER AND EMBEZZLEMENT OF REGIMENTAL FUNDS. COMING WEST.

LEO D'ARCY,
COL., 12th CAVALRY.

Without comment I handed the message to Chapin, who read it aloud. Moira's face paled, but she said nothing.

"I remember the case," Chapin said. "Park Cantwell was a captain in the cavalry. He embezzled some twenty thousand dollars, and when faced with the charge, murdered his commanding officer and escaped. He was captured, then broke jail, and killed two more men getting away. He was last heard of five or six years ago in Mexico."

"Any chance of a mistake?"

"I don't think so."

Chapin glanced down at the message. "May I have this? I'll take it to Sheriff Tharp."

"What is it Park and Booker want?" Canaval said.

"Lyell said Park wanted money, quick money. How he planned to get it . . . that's the question."

Moira had not looked at me. Several times I tried to catch her eye, but she avoided my glance. Whether or not she believed I had killed her father, she obviously wanted no part of me.

Canaval's hoarse breathing was the only sound in the quiet room. Outside in the mesquite I could hear a cicada singing. It was hot and still. . . .

Discouraged, I turned toward the door. Canaval stopped me.

"Where to now?"

Back to the Two-Bar? There was nothing there to

be done now, and there were things to be done else-where. Then, suddenly, I knew where I was going. There was a thing that had to be done, and had to be done before I would feel that I could face myself. It was a thing that must not be left undone.

"To see Morgan Park."

Moira turned, her lips forming an unspoken protest.

"Don't . . . I've seen him kill a man with his fists," Chapin protested.

"He won't kill me."

"What is this?" Moira's voice was scathing. "A cheap, childish desire for revenge? Or just talk? You've no right to go to town and start trouble! You've no reason to start a fight with Morgan Park just because he beat you once!"

"Protecting him?" My voice was not pleasant. I did not feel pleasant.

Did she, I wonder, actually love the man? Had I been that mistaken? The more I thought of that, the angrier I became.

"No! I'm not protecting him! From what I saw after the first fight, it is you who will need protection!"

She could have said nothing more likely to bring all my determination to the surface.

Her eyes were wide, her face white. For an instant we stared at each other, and then I turned on my heel and went out of the house, and the door slammed behind me.

Buck sensed my mood, and he was moving even as I gathered the reins. When my leg swung over the saddle he was already running.

So I would need protection, would I? Anger tore at me, and I swore bitterly as the buckskin leaned into the wind. Mad all the way through, I was eager for any kind of a fight, wanting to slash, to destroy.

And perhaps it was fortunate for me that I was in such a mood when I rounded a bend and rode right into the middle of Slade and his men.

They had not heard me. The shoulder of rock and

the blowing wind kept the sound from them. Suddenly they were set upon by a charging rider who rode right into them, and even as their startled heads swung on their shoulders my horse smashed between two of the riders, sending both staggering for footing. As the buckskin struck Slade's horse with his shoulder, I drew my gun and slashed out and down with the barrel. It caught the nearest rider over the ear and he went off his horse as if struck by lightning. Swinging around, I blasted the gun from the fist of another rider with a quick shot. Slade was fighting his maddened, frantic horse, and I leaned over and hit it a slap with my hat.

The horse gave a tremendous leap and started to run like a scared rabbit, with Slade fighting to stay in the saddle. He had lost a stirrup when my horse struck his and hadn't recovered it. The last I saw of him was his running horse and a cloud of dust.

It all had happened in a split second. My advantage was that I had come upon them fighting mad and ready to strike out at anything, everything.

The fourth man had been maneuvering for a shot at me but was afraid to risk it for fear of hitting a companion in the whirling turmoil of men and horses. As I wheeled, we both fired and both missed. He tried to steady his horse Buck did not like any of it and was fighting to get away. I let him have his head, snapping a quick backward shot at the man in the saddle. It must have clipped his ear, for he ducked like a bee-stung farmer, and then Buck was laying them down on the trail for town.

Feeding shells into my gun, I let him go, feeling better for the action, ready for anything. The town loomed up and I raced my horse down the street and swung off, leaving him with the hostler to cool off and be rubbed down.

One look at me and Katie O'Hara knew I was spoiling for trouble.

"Morgan Park is in town," she warned me. "Over at the saloon."

It was all I wanted to know. Turning, I walked across the street. I was mad clear through, stirred up by the action, and ready for more of it. I wanted the man who had struck me down without warning, and I wanted him badly. It was a job I had to do if I was going to be able to live with myself.

Morgan Park was there, all right. He was seated at a table with Jake Booker. Evidently, with Maclaren dead and Canaval shot down, they figured it was safe to come out in the open.

I wasted no time. "Booker," I said, "you're a no-account, sheep-stealin' shyster, but I've heard you're smart. You should be too smart to do business with a thief and a murderer."

It caught them flat-footed, and before either could move I grabbed the table and swung it out of the way, and then I slapped Morgan Park across the face with my hat.

He came off his chair with an inarticulate roar and I met him with a left that flattened his lip against his teeth. Blood showered from the cut and I threw a right, high and hard.

It caught him on the chin and he stopped dead in his tracks.

He blinked, and then he came on. I doubt if the thought that he might be whipped had ever occurred to him. He rushed, swinging those huge, iron-like fists. One of them caught me on the skull and rang bells in my head. Another dug for my midsection, but my elbow blocked the blow. Turning, I took a high right over my shoulder, then threw him bodily into the bar rail.

He came up with a lunge and I nailed him with a left as he reached his feet. The blow spatted into his face with a wicked sound, and there was a line of red from the broken skin. He hit me with both hands then and I felt that old smoky taste in my mouth as I walked in, blasting with both fists.

He swung a right and I went under it with a hooked left to the belly, then rolled at the hips and drove my right to the same spot. He grunted and I tried to step back, but he was too fast and too strong. He moved in on me and I hit him a raking blow to the face before we clinched. His arms went around me but I dug my head under his chin and bowed my back. It stopped him, and we stood toe to toe, wrestling on our feet. He got his arms lower and heaved me high. I smashed him in the face with my right as he threw me.

Just as he let go I grabbed a handful of hair with my right hand and he screamed. We hit the floor together, and rolling over, I beat him to my feet.

There was a crowd around us now, but although they were yelling, I heard no sound. I walked in, weaving to miss his haymakers, but he jarred me with a right to the head, then a short left. He knocked me back against the bar and grabbed a bottle. He swung at my head, but I went under it and butted him in the chest. He went down, and my momentum carried me past him.

He sprang up and I hit him. He turned halfway around, and when he did I sprang to his shoulders and jammed both spurs into his thighs. He screamed with agony and ducked. I went over his head, landing on all fours, and he kicked me rolling.

Coming up, we circled. Both of us were wary now. My hot anger was gone. This was a fight for my life, and I could win only if I used every bit of wit and cunning I possessed.

His shirt was in ribbons. I'd never seen the man stripped before, and he had the chest and shoulders of a giant. He came at me and I nailed him with a left and then we stood swinging with both hands, toe to toe. His advantage in size and weight was more than balanced by my superior speed.

I circled, feinted, and when he swung, I smashed a right to his belly. An instant later I did it again. Then I threw a left to his battered features, and when his arms came up I smashed both hands to the body. Again and again I hit him in the stomach. He slowed, tried to set himself, but I knocked his left up and hit him in the solar plexus with a right. He grunted, and for the first time his knees sagged. Standing wide-legged, I pumped blows at his head and body as hard as I could swing. He tried to grab at me. Setting myself, I threw that right, high and hard.

My fist caught him on the side of the chin as he started to step in. He stopped, swayed, then fell, crashing through the swinging doors and rolling over to the edge of the porch, where he lay, sprawled out cold.

Turning from the door, I took the glass of whiskey somebody handed to me, and gulped it down. My heart was pounding and my body was glistening with sweat and blood. My breath came in great gasps and I sagged against the bar, trying to recover.

Somebody yelled something, and I turned. Morgan Park was standing there, his feet spread. As I turned, he hit me. It was flush on the chin and it felt like a blow from an axe. I fell back against the bar, my head spinning, and as I fought for consciousness, I stared down at his feet, amazed that such a huge man could have such small feet.

He hit me again and I went down, and then he kicked at my head with those deadly, narrow-toed boots. Only the roll of my head saved me as the kick glanced off my skull.

It was my turn to be down and out. Then somebody drenched me with a bucket of water and I sat up. It was Moira who had thrown the water.

I was too dazed to wonder how she came to be there, then somebody said, "There he is!" I saw Park standing there with his hands on his hips, leering at me through his broken lips.

We went for each other again and how we did it I'll never know. Both of us had already taken a terrific beating. But I had to whip Morgan Park or kill him with my bare hands.

Toe to toe we slugged it out, then I took a quick step back and when he came after me, I nailed him with a right uppercut. He staggered, and I hit him again.

"Stop it, you crazy fools! Stop it or I'll throw you both in jail!"

Sheriff Will Tharp stood in the door with a gun on us. His cold blue eyes meant what he said.

Around him were at least twenty men. Key Chapin was there ... and Bodie Miller.

Park backed toward the door, then turned away. He looked punch drunk.

After that I spent an hour bathing my face in hot water.

Then I went to the livery stable and crawled into the loft, taking with me a blanket and my rifle. I had worn my guns all along.

Outside somebody moved and murmured in the street. Below me the horses stamped and chomped their feed. Slowly, my exhausted muscles relaxed, my fists came unknotted, and I slept ...

NINETEEN

WHEN I AWAKENED, BRIGHT SUNLIGHT was filtering through a couple of cracks in the roof, and I lay there, feeling soreness in every muscle. I watched the motes dancing in the stream of light and then rolled over.

The loft was like an oven. Sitting up, I gingerly

touched my face with my fingers. It was swollen and sore. Working my fingers to loosen them up, I heard a movement on the ladder. Looking over my shoulder, I saw Morgan Park staring at me. And I knew that I looked into the eyes of a man who was no longer sane.

He stood there, his head and shoulders visible above the loft floor, and I could see the hatred in his eyes. He made no move, just looked at me, and I knew then he had come to kill me.

I could have knocked him off the ladder. I could have cooled him, but I could not take that advantage. This was one man, sane or insane, whom I had to whip fairly or I would never be quite comfortable again. There was no reason in it. He had taken advantage of me . . . it was simply the way I felt.

Poised for instant movement, I knew I was in trouble. I knew now what enormous vitality that huge body held, and that he could move with amazing speed for his size.

When he came off the ladder, I got to my feet. When he moved I could see he was stiff, also. Yet I was in better shape. My workouts with Mulvaney had prepared me for this.

He did not rush me when he had his feet on the loft floor. He just stood there with his hands on his hips, looking at me. And the advantage was with him.

One side of the loft, where the ladder was, opened to the barn. A fall from there would cripple a man. The rest of the loft, except for a few square feet, was stacked with hay. With his size and weight, in these close quarters, the advantage was on his side.

My mouth was dry and I dearly wanted a drink. He faced me, and I knew at the instant when he was going to move. He came toward me, not fast, taking his time. Morgan Park had come for the kill.

He moved closer, and I struck out. He took the blow on his shoulder and kept coming in, forcing me back into the hay. Suddenly he lunged and swung. I rolled inside the punch but his weight knocked me back into the hay, for I could put no power into my punches.

With cold brutality he began to swing, his eyes lit up with sadistic delight. Lights exploded in my head, and then another punch hit me, and another.

Deliberately I slid down the side of the hay, and threw my weight against his legs. He staggered and, unable to reach me, backed off a step and swung his leg to kick. I threw my shoulder into him, and he fell back to the floor. Jumping past him, I grabbed a rope and slid down to the barn floor.

He turned and started down the ladder. Near the door I heard someone yell. "They're at it again!" And then Morgan Park came for me.

Now it had to be ended, once and for all. Moving away from his first punch, I stabbed a left to his cut mouth, starting the blood again. He was slower than he had been yesterday, and the blood seemed to bother him. I feinted, then hit him solidly in the ribs. Rolling at the hips, I threw three solid punches to the midsection before he grabbed me, then I twisted away and hit him in the face.

He seemed puzzled. He wanted to kill, but I was being careful to avoid his hands. He swung, and I slipped inside the punch with a right to the chin.

He stopped, and I stepped in wide-legged and hit him with both fists on the chin, and he went down. I stepped back and allowed him to rise.

Behind me a crowd had gathered, but it was a silent crowd this time, a crowd awed by what they were seeing.

Morgan Park got up, and when he came off the floor he rushed, head down and swinging. Side-stepping swiftly, I thrust out a foot and he tripped, falling heavily. He got up again, stolidly, with determination. When he turned toward me, I hit him.

The blow struck his chin solidly, like the butt of an axe striking a log. He fell, not backwards, but on his face. He lay there quiet and unmoving, and I knew my fight was over.

Sodden with weariness and for once fed up with fighting, I picked up my hat and walked by the silent men. I got my rifle again and shoved it in my saddle boot. Nobody said anything, but they stared at my battered face and torn clothing.

At the door I met Sheriff Will Tharp coming in. He stopped, measuring me. "Didn't I tell you to stop fighting in this town, Brennan?"

"What am I to do? Let him beat my head off? He followed me here."

"Better have some rest," Tharp said then. "When you're rested, ride out of town for a while."

When I was in the doorway, he stopped me again. "I'm arresting Park for murder. I have official confirmation on your message."

All I wanted just then was a drink of cold water. Gallons of it.

Yet all the way to Mother O'Hara's I kept remembering that bucket of water dashed over me in the saloon. Had that really been Moira, or had it been an illusion?

When I had washed my face and patched my shirt together I went into the restaurant. Key Chapin was there.

He said little, watching me eat, passing things to me. My jaw was sore and I ate carefully.

"Booker's still in town," Chapin said. "What's he want?"

Right then I didn't care. But as I drank my coffee, I began to wonder. This was my country now, my home. It did matter to me, and Moira mattered.

"Was I crazy, or was Moira in there last night?"

"She was there, all right."

Refilling my cup, I thought that over. She was not entirely against me then.

"You'd better get over to Doc West's. That face needs some attention."

Out in the air I felt better. With food and some black coffee inside me I felt like a new man. The mountain air was fresh and good to the taste, and even the sun felt good.

I walked along the street .Out of the grab bag of the world I had picked this town. Here in this place I had elected to remain, to put down my roots, to build a ranch. Old man Ball had given me a ranch, and I had given my word. Here I could cease being a trouble-hunting, rambunctious young rider and settle down to a citizen's life. It was time for that, but I wanted one more thing. I wanted Moira.

Doc West lived in a small white cottage surrounded by rose bushes. Tall poplars stood in the woodyard and there was a patch of lawn inside the white picket fence. It was the only painted fence in town.

A tall, austere man with a shock of graying hair answered the door. He smiled at me.

"No doubt about who you are, Brennan. I just came from treating the other man."

"How is he?"

"Three broken ribs and a broken jaw. The ribs were broken last night, I'd say."

"There was no quit in him."

"He's a dangerous man, Brennan. He's still dangerous."

After he had checked me over and patched up my face, I got back on my feet and buckled on my guns. My fingers were stiff. I kept working them, trying to loosen up the muscles. What if I met Jim Pinder now? Or that weasel, Bodie Miller?

Picking up my sombrero, I remembered something. "Have Tharp check Morgan Park's boots with those tracks Canaval found. I'm betting they'll fit."

"You think he killed Maclaren?"

"Yes."

On the porch I stopped, gingerly trying to fit my hat over the lumps on my skull. It wasn't easy.

Scissors snipped among the rose bushes. Turning I looked into the eyes of Moira Maclaren.

Her dark hair was piled on her head, the first time I had seen it that way. And I decided right then it was much the best way.

"How's Canaval?" I asked.

"Better. Fox is running the ranch."

"He's a good man."

My hat was back in my hands. I turned it around. Neither of us seemed to want to say what we were thinking. I was thinking that I loved her, but I was afraid to say it.

"You're staying on at the Two-Bar?"

"The house is finished." When I said that, I looked at her. "It's finished . . . but it's empty."

Her voice faltered a little, and she snipped at a rose, cutting the stem much too short.

"You . . . you aren't living in it?"

"Yes, I'm there, but you aren't."

So there it was, out in the open again. I turned my hat again and looked down at my boots. They were scuffed and lost to color.

"You shouldn't say that. We can't mean anything to each other. You . . . you're a killer. I watched you fight. You actually *like* it."

Thinking it over, I had to agree.

"Why not? I'm a man . . . and fighting has been man's work for a long time on this earth."

"It's bad . . . it will always be bad."

I turned my hat, then put it on. "Maybe . . . but as long as there are men like Morgan Park, Jim Pinder, and Bodie Miller, there must be men to stand against them."

She looked up quickly. "But why does it have to be you? Matt, don't fight any more! Please don't!"

I drew back a little, though I wanted to go to her and take her in my arms.

"There's Bodie Miller. Unless someone kills him first, I'll have to face him."

"But you don't have to!" Her eyes flashed angrily. "All that's so silly! Why should you?"

"Because I'm a man. I can't live in a woman's world. I must live with men, and be judged by men. If I back down from Miller, I'll be through here. And Miller will go on to kill other men."

"You can go away! You can go to California to straighten out some business for me! Matt, you could—

"No, I'm staying here."

There were more words, and they were hard words, and then we parted, no better off.

But she had started me thinking about Bodie Miller. He was riding his luck with spurs, and he would be hunting me. Remembering that sallow-faced killer, I knew we couldn't live in the same country without meeting. And my hands were bruised, my fingers stiff.

Bodie Miller was full of salt now. I'd have to ride the country always ready. One moment off guard and I would have no other moments, ever.

How could I live and not kill?

Yet when I rode up to the ranch I was thinking of a dark-haired girl tall among the roses. . . .

TWENTY

JONATHAN BENARAS STARED AT MY face, then looked away, not wanting to embarrass me with questions.

"It was quite a fight . . . he took a licking."

Benaras grinned in his slow way, and a sly humor flickered in his gray eyes. "If he looks worse'n you do, he must be a sight."

While I stripped the saddle from the buckskin I told

them what had happened, as briefly as possible. They listened, and I could see they were pleased. Jolly hunkered down near the barn and watched me.

"It'll please Pa . . . he never set much store by Morgan Park."

"Wish I'd been there to see it," Mulvaney mused. "It must have been a sweet fight."

We went inside where supper was laid, and we sat at a table and ate as men should—for the first time, not around a campfire. But I was thinking of the girl I wanted at this table, and the life I wanted to build with her, and how she would have none of me.

Nobody talked. The fire crackled on the hearth, and there was a subdued rattle of dishes. When we had eaten, Jolly Benaras went out into the dark with his rifle. Walking to the veranda, I looked down the dark valley.

The first thing was to find out what Booker and Morgan had been up to, and the only possible clue I had was the silver assay.

The place to look was where the Two-Bar and the Boxed M joined, I decided. The next day I would ride that way, and see for myself. If it was not there, then I must swing ride and need tracks, for tracks there must be.

Mulvaney rode with me at daybreak. The Irishman had a facile mind, and a shrewd one. He was a good man to have on such a search, and also, he had mined and knew a little about ore.

The morning fell behind us with the trail we made across the Dark Canyon Plateau, and we lost it at Fable Canyon's rim. Off on our right, but far away, lay the Sweet Alice Hills.

Heat waves danced. . . . I mopped my face and neck. We saw no tracks but those of deer, and once those of a lobo wolf.

We rode right and left, searching. More deer . . . the spoor of a mountain sheep, the drying hide of an antelope, with a few scattered bones, gnawed by wolf teeth. And then I saw something else. . . .

Fresh tracks of a shod horse.

Turning in my saddle, I lifted my hat and waved. It was a minute before Mulvaney saw me, and then he turned his mule and rode toward me at a shambling trot. When he came closer I showed him the tracks.

"Maybe a couple of hours old," he said.

"One of the Slade gang?" I suggested, but I did not believe it.

We fell into the trail and followed along, not talking. At one place a hoof had slipped and the torn earth had not yet dried out. Obviously then, the horse had passed after the sun had left the trail, possibly within the past hour. The earth had dried some, but not entirely.

We rode rapidly, but with increasing care. Within an hour we knew we were gaining. When the canyon branched we found where the rider had filled his canteen and prepared his meal.

We looked at his fire and we knew more about him. The man was not a Slade, for the Slades were good men on a trail, and their gang were men on the dodge who had ridden the wild country. The maker of the fire had used some wood that burned badly, and his fire was in a place where the slightest breeze would swirl smoke in his face.

The boot tracks were small. Near by there was the butt of a cigar, chewed some, and only half smoked through.

Cowhands rarely smoke cigars, and they know which wood will burn well and which will not. And they have learned about fires by building many.

When we started to go, we suddenly stopped. For there were no tracks.

He had come here, watered his horse, prepared a meal, then disappeared.

The rock walls offered no escape. The earth around

the spring was undisturbed beyond a few square yards. The tracks led in ... and none led out.

"We've trailed a ghost," Mulvaney said, and I almost agreed.

"We'd best think of him as a man. What would a man do?"

"Not even a snake could mount those cliffs, so if he rode in, he rode out."

There were no tracks, nothing had been brushed out. We scouted up the canyons, but we found nothing. Mulvaney tried one branch, and I the other.

Walking my buckskin, I studied the ground with care. Wild horses had fed up this canyon, browsing along slowly, evidently at least twenty in the group. Suddenly the character of the tracks changed. The horses had broken into a wild run!

Studying the hoof prints, I could see no indication of any tracks other than those of the wild horses.

What was likely to frighten them? A grizzly? Perhaps, but they were rarely seen this far south. A wolf—no. A wild stallion was not likely to be disturbed by a wolf, even a large one. Nor was a wolf likely to get himself into a fight with a wild stallion in such close quarters. A lion then? Certainly, a lion perched on one of these cliffs might make an easy kill. Yet no lion would make them run as they had. The horses would move off all right, but not in such wild flight.

Only one thing was likely to make them run as they had ... a man.

The tracks were only a few hours old at most. They might even be less than an hour old.

And then I saw something that alerted me instantly. In tracking, what the tracker seeks for is the thing out of place, the thing that does not belong. And on a manzanita bush was a bit of sheep's wool!

Dismounting, I plucked it from the bush. It was not the wool from a wild sheep, not from a bighorn. This was wool from a merino, a good sheep, too.

No sheep would ever find their way into this wild canyon alone, and who would bring them in and why?

The whole situation became suddenly plain. The man we had followed had tied sheepskin over his horse's hoofs so they would leave no tracks.

Mulvaney was waiting for me when I rode back. I showed him the wool and explained quickly.

"A good idea ... but we'll get him now."

The way out through the branch canyon led northeast, and finally to a high, windswept plateau unbroken by anything but a few towering rocks and low growing sagebrush. We sat our horses, squinting against the distance.

Far off the Blue Mountains lifted their lofty summits ten thousand feet into the sky, but even those summits gathered no clouds. And between us and the mountains was a Dante's *Inferno* of unbelievable grandeur, arid and empty.

"We may never find him," Mulvaney said at last. "You could lose an army out there."

"We'll find him."

Taking my hat from my head, I mopped my brow, then wiped the hatband. My eyes squinted against the glare. Sweat got into the corner of one eye and it smarted. My face felt raw and sore. We rode on into the heat, the only sounds those made by our walking horses; the only change, the distant shadows in the canyon and hollows of the distant hills.

Some of this country I had known, much of it had been described to me by old man Ball or the Benaras boys, who were among the few white men to have ridden into this desolate waste. Far away, between us and the bulk of the mountains, I could see a rim. That would be Salt Creek Mesa, with the towering finger above it, Cathedral Butte. Far beyond, and even higher, but not appearing so at this distance, was Shay Mountain.

The man we were searching for was somewhere in

the maze of canyons between us and those mountains. And he could not be far ahead.

With the sheepskin on his horse's hoofs he would leave no trail but, knowing what to look for, we might find some indication of his passing. And his horse could not move fast.

We rode on, walking our horses. The heat was deadening, the plodding pace of the horses almost hypnotic. I shook my head, and dried my hands on my shirt.

Mulvaney's face was hard and sweaty. There was deep sunburn along his cheekbones and jaw. He rolled a smoke and lighted it, clipping the cigarette tight between his flat lips, marked with old scars.

"Hell of a country!"

His eyes flickered at me. "Yeah." He shook his canteen to guage the amount of water remaining, then rinsed his mouth, holding the water a while before he swallowed. My own thirst seemed intensified by hearing that slosh of water in his canteen. I took a long swallow from my own.

After I replaced the cork my eyes swept the country, searching it far away, then nearer, nearer.

Nothing. . . .

We went on, seeing another bit of wool, and later a smudged place in the dust.

Not far . . . he ain't far."

Mulvaney was right. We were closing in. But who were we following? What manner of man was this? Not a plainsman, not a cowhand. Yet a man who knew something of the wilds, and a man who was cunning and wary.

I mopped my face again, and swore softly at the heat. Sweat trickled down my ribs and I rubbed my horse's neck and spoke reassuringly.

"We'll need water," Mulvaney said.

"Yes."

"So will he."

"Maybe he knows where it is. He isn't riding blind."

"No."

Our talk lapsed and we rode on, our bodies moving to the rhythm of the walking horses. . . . The sun declined a little. It must be midafternoon, or later. I wanted another drink, but did not dare take it. I wanted to dismount for a pebble to put in my mouth, but the effort seemed too much.

Our senses were lulled by the heat and the easy movement. We rode half dozing in our saddles.

And then there was a shot.

It slapped sharply across our consciousness, and we reined wide, putting our mounts apart.

We had heard no bullet, only the flat, hard report, not far away. And then another.

"He ain't shootin' at us."

"Let's get off the flat . . . *quick!*"

The shots had come from the canyon, the trail led there, so we went over the edge into the depths, and swung, right, always right, down the switchback trail.

If we were seen here we were dead, caught flat against the mountainside like paper ducks pinned to a wall.

TWENTY-ONE

AT THE BOTTOM WE SWUNG OUR HORSES in a swirl of dust and leaped them for cover in a thick cluster of trees and brush. Even our horses felt the tension as they stood, heads up and alert.

All was still. Some distance away a stone rattled. Sweat trickled behind my ear and I smelled the hot aroma of dust and sun-baked leaves. My palms grew sweaty and I dried them, but there was no further sound.

Careful to let my saddle creak as little as possible, I swung down, Winchester in hand, and with a motion to Mulvaney to stay put, I moved away through the brush.

From the edge of the trees I could see no more than thirty yards in one direction, no more than twenty in the other. Rock walls towered and the canyon sand lay still under the blazing sun. Close against the walls there was a thin strip of shadow.

Somewhere near by water trickled, aggravating my thirst. My neck felt hot and sticky, my shirt clung to my shoulders. Shifting the rifle in my hands, I studied the rock wall with misgiving. I dried my hands on my jeans and, taking a chance, moved out from my cover, and into that six-inch band of shade against the wall. Easing along to a bend in the wall, I peered around the corner.

Sixty yards away stood a saddled horse, head hanging. My eyes searched and saw nothing more, and then just visible beyond a white, water-worn boulder, I saw a boot and a leg as far as the knee.

For a space of a minute I watched it. There was no movement, no sound. Cautiously, wary for a trick, I advanced, ready to fire. Only the occasional chuckle of water over rocks broke the stillness. And then I saw the dead man.

That he was quite dead was beyond doubt. His skull was bloody and there was a bullet hole over one eye. He probably never knew what hit him. It served also as a warning. A man who could shoot like that was nobody to trifle with.

There was a vague familiarity to him, and moving nearer, I saw his skull bore a swelling. This had been the rider with Slade whom I had slugged on the trail.

The bullet had struck over the eye and ranged downward, which indicated he had been shot from ambush, perhaps from somewhere on the canyon wall. Lining up the probable position, I sighted a tuft of green on the wall that might be a ledge.

At my low call, Mulvaney approached. He studied the man.

"This wasn't the man we followed."

"One of the Slade crowd," I told him.

We started on, but no longer were the tracks disguised. The man we followed was going more slowly now.

Suddenly, there was a boot print, sharp and clear. Something turned over inside me.

"Mulvaney, that's the track of the man who shot Maclaren!"

"But Morgan Park's in jail," he protested, studying the track. He knew that I had ridden by to see the track Canaval had mentioned.

"He was—"

My buckskin's head came up, his nostrils dilated. Grabbing his nose, I stifled the whinny. Then I followed his gaze.

Less than a hundred yards away a strange dun horse was picketed near a clump of bunchgrass.

"You know," I said thoughtfully, "whoever we followed may think he has killed whoever followed him. He may think he's safe now."

We hid our horses in a box canyon and climbed the wall for a look around. From the top of the mesa we could see all the surrounding country. Under the southern edge of the wall opposite was a cluster of ancient ruins, beyond them deep canyons.

I studied the terrain ahead, and suddenly saw a man emerge from a crack in the earth, carrying a heavy sack. He placed it on the ground and removed his coat, then with a pick and a bar he began working at a slab over the crack from which he had come.

Mulvaney could see the man, but not what he was doing.

Explaining as I watched, I saw him take the bar

and pry hard at the slab. The rock slid, then came all the way, carrying with it a pile of debris. The dust rose, settled. The crack was invisible.

After carefully looking to either side, the man concealed his tools, picked up his rifle and the sack, and started back toward us. Studying him as he walked, I could see he wore black jeans, very dusty now, and a small hat. His face was not visible, but he bore no resemblance to anyone I knew.

He disappeared from sight, and for a long time we heard no sound.

We had been concealed from sight, or so we believed, but now we climbed back down to the canyon floor. We were turning toward the box canyon where our horses were hidden when we heard two shots in quick succession.

We stared at each other, puzzled. But there was no other sound as we uneasily worked our way back to the box canyon.

Mulvaney saw it first, and he swore viciously. It was the first time I had ever heard him swear.

My horse and his mule lay sprawled in pools of their own blood. Our canteens had been emptied and smashed with stones. We were thirty miles from the nearest ranch, and our way lay through some of the most rugged country on earth.

"There's water, but no way to carry it. Do you think he knew who we were?"

"If he lives in this country he should know that buckskin of mine," I said bitterly. "He was the best horse I ever owned."

It told me something else about our man, whoever he was. He was utterly ruthless. This man had not driven the horses off, he had shot them down. He was cautious, too. To have hunted us down might have exposed himself to danger.

"We'll have a look at the place he covered up. No use leaving without that."

It was almost dark before we had dug enough

behind the slab of rock to get at the secret. Mulvaney cut into the rock with his pick. Ripping out a chunk he showed it to me, his eyes glowing with excitement.

"Silver! The biggest strike I ever saw! Better than Silver Reef!"

The ore glittered in his hand as he turned it. This was what had killed Rud Maclaren and the others.

"It's rich," I said, "but I'd settle for the Two-Bar."

"But it's a handsome sight!"

"Pocket it then. We've a long walk."

"Now?"

"Tonight ... while it's cool."

The shadows grew long while we walked, and thick blackness came down to choke the canyons and cover the mountains. We walked on, with little talk, up Ruin Canyon and over a saddle of the Sweet Alice Hills and down to a spring on the far side.

There we rested and drank, and I was remembering, and thinking ahead.

The camp where I had seen Slade's gang was not many miles away, it had water and shelter, and so far as they knew only Morgan Park knew about it. Outlaws are rarely energetic men, and I doubted that they had moved. Where outlaws were, there would be horses also.

It had taken us five hours to walk ten miles, and it was well into the night. Most of our walking had been along the canyon's bottom. Now we would be crossing Dark Canyon Platau . . . but no, *this* was the canyon they were in!

Dark it was as we walked, doing no talking. There was water rustling over stones and the dampness in the canyon was good after the heat of the long day.

We heard singing before we saw the light of the fire. The canyon walls caught and magnified the sound. A few yards further along, we spotted the fire, and the reflection of it on a face.

Three men were there, and one sang as he cleaned his rifle.

We were at the edge of the firelight before they saw us, and I had my Winchester on them, and Mulvaney his cannon-like four-shot pistol.

Slade was no fool. He sat very still, with his hands in sight. His face was pale, as well it might be, with a hanging waiting for him.

"Who is it?"

Our faces were shielded by the brims of our hats, and we stood partly concealed by the brush.

"The name is Matt Brennan, and I'm not asking for trouble. We want two good horses. You can lend them or we'll take them.

"Our horses," I added, "were shot by the same man who killed your partner."

"Lott killed?"

Slade studied me, absorbing that news. None of them seemed in the mood for trouble. Nevertheless I discouraged any such idea with my Winchester.

"He met up with a man we were trailing. He caught a slug between the eyes." I pushed my hand up and moved my hat back. "Then he shot both our horses."

"Damn a man who'll kill a horse. Who was it?"

"He leaves a track like Morgan Park, but Park's in jail."

"Not now," Slade said. "He broke jail within an hour after dark last night. Pulled an iron bar out of that old wall, stole a horse, and disappeared."

But the man we had seen had not been big enough for Park. Nevertheless, it was a thing to remember.

"How about the horses?"

"Take them. We're clearing out."

"Are they spares?"

"We've got a dozen extras. In our business it pays to keep fresh horses." He grinned up at me and slowly leaned back on his elbow. "No hard feelin's, Brennan?"

"None . . . only be careful."

"With two guns on us? Sure. . . . What kind of a cannon is that your partner's got? A man could ride into that barrel with his hat on."

Mulvaney went after the horses, then returned with them. They were saddled and bridled.

Slade's mouth twisted when he saw the saddles. But he had nothing to say.

"Any other news?"

He smiled maliciously at me. "Yeah. Bodie Miller's talking it big around town. Says you're his meat."

"He's a heavy eater, that boy. Hope he doesn't tackle anything that'll give him indigestion."

We mounted up. "The horses will be at the livery stable in town."

"Better not," Slade said. "There's a corral in the woods back of Armstrong's. You might leave them there."

The horses were fresh and ready to run, and we let them go. It was good to be in the saddle again, but both of us were hanging heavy before many miles.

We rode and we did not talk, for neither of us had words to say. The stars faded and the sky turned gray in the east. and then a pale yellow showed above the mountains behind us. The rosy color of dawn tipped the mountains before us, and we slowed our pace and cantered down the trail and watched the sun pick out the roofs ahead of us.

Daylight saw us riding down the street at Hattan's Point.

TWENTY-TWO

WE FOUND A TOWN THAT WAS SILENT and waiting. But the loft was full of hay and both of us needed sleep. And what was to come would wait.

Two hours later, as if by signal, I awakened suddenly. Leaving Mulvaney to his needed rest, I splashed water on my face and headed for Mother O'Hara's. The first person I saw when I came through the door was Moira. And the second was Key Chapin.

"Sorry," Chapin said. "We just heard the news."

My blank expression must have told him. I knew of no news, but I didn't want to wait to hear it.

"You're losing the Two-Bar."

"What are you talking about?"

"Jake Booker filed a deed to the Two-Bar. He purchased all rights from a nephew of old man Ball's. He had laid claim to the Boxed M, maintains it was never actually owned by Rud Maclaren, but belonged to his brother-in-law, now dead. Booker found a relative of the brother-in-law, and bought the property."

"It's a steal."

"If he goes to court he can make it very rough."

He went on to explain that Booker was a shrewd lawyer, and despite my two witnesses, could go far toward establishing a solid claim.

He went on to say that Booker had turned up the fact that a few years before, while suffering from a gunshot wound, Maclaren had deeded the ranch to his brother-in-law and it had apparently never been deeded back to himself.

Moira's face looked pale, and I could understand

why. If Booker could make his claim hold good, then Moira, instead of being an independent young lady with a cattle ranch, would be broke and hunting a job. I knew that Maclaren had spent cash in developing the place and actually had little money on hand.

"What's more important right now," Chapin added, "Booker has a court order impounding all bank deposits, stopping all sales, and freezing everything as is until the case is settled."

I sat down. Swiftly, I ordered my thoughts. Booker would have paid out no money for claims he did not think he could substantiate in court. The man was shrewd.

There was no attorney within miles capable of coping with Booker. What had begun as a range war had degenerated into a grand steal by a shyster lawyer. And neither of us would have the money to fight him.

A thought occurred to me. "Has Canaval been told?"

Chapin gestured impatiently. "There's nothing he can do. He's only a foreman."

Katie O'Hara brought me coffee and it tasted good.

Sheriff Will Tharp had left town, accompanied by the recently arrived Colonel D'Arcy. They had gone to Morgan Park's ranch, searching for him.

"They should have gone to Dark Canyon," I said.

"Why there?" Chapin looked at me curiously. "What would take a man there?"

"That's where he'll be."

When Katie O'Hara brought my breakfast I ate in silence. Morgan Park was free and would be wanting a shot at me. Bodie Miller was probably in town. Whatever was to be done would have to be done fast, and however good I might be with gun or fists, I had no experience with the intricacies of the law. I could not hope to meet Booker on his own ground.

Moira did not look at me. She talked a little with Key Chapin, who had been her father's friend.

"Moira," I said, "you better send a messenger to the ranch to tell Canaval what's happened."

Still she did not look at me. "What can he do? It would only worry him."

"No matter—take my advice."

She tightened a little, resenting the suggestion. "Better still, have Fox and some of your boys bring him into town in a buckboard."

"But I don't—

"Do what I say." My abruptness seemed to shock her. She looked up, and our eyes met. Hers fell swiftly, but for an instant I thought . . .

"Moira," I said gently, "you want your ranch. It can be saved. Get Canaval in here and tell him what's happened. Have witnesses, take a statement from him, and have it signed by the witnesses."

"What are you talking about? What statement?"

"Do what I advise."

Finishing my coffee with a gulp, I picked up my hat and put it on the back of my head. Then I rolled a smoke. While I was doing it, my eyes were studying the street out side. There was no sign of Miller.

But then I saw something else. A weary dun horse was tied to the side of the corral. It was barely visible between the buildings.

"Who owns that horse?"

Chapin came to the window to look. He shook his head. "I've no idea."

Katie was picking up the dishes, and she glanced out the window. "Jake Booker rides it. He did this morning."

And Jake Booker had small feet.

Mulvaney was crawling down from the loft when I got to him. He listened, then ran to the stable office and got a fresh horse.

Key Chapin was in the door of the restaurant when I walked by.

"Get Canaval in here. We're having a showdown. Send for Jim Pinder, too."

He studied me. "Matt, what do you know?"

"Enough . . . I think. Enough to save the Boxed M and probably to find the man who killed Maclaren."

Without waiting, I went through the town, store by store, saloon by saloon. I was looking for Bodie Miller, but there was no sign of him, nor of his partner.

At Mother O'Hara's, Key Chapin and Moira were waiting. I sat down and without giving them a chance to talk, I outlined my plan in as few words as possible. Moira listened with surprise, I thought, but she shouldn't have been surprised, for I had said much of this before. Chapin nodded from time to time.

"It might work." he agreed at last. "We can try."

"What about Tharp?"

"He'll stand with us. He's a solid man, Matt."

"All right, then. Showdown in the morning."

The voice came from behind me. It was a voice I knew, low, confident, a little mocking.

"Why, sure! Showdown in the morning, I'd like that, Brennan."

It was Bodie Miller.

He was smiling when I looked at him, but his eyes did not join in the smile.

This was Bodie, the man who wanted to kill me. . . . Bodie the killer.

The sun in the morning came up clear and hot. At daybreak the sky was without a cloud, and the distant mountains shimmered in a haze of their own making. The desert lost itself in heat waves, and a stillness lay upon both desert and town, a sort of poised awareness that seemed to walk on tiptoe as if the slightest sound might shatter it."

When I emerged on the street I was a man alone. The street was empty as a town of ghosts, silent except for the sound of my own boots on the board walk. Then, as if that sound had broken the spell, the bartender came from the saloon and began to sweep off the walk in front.

He glanced at me, bobbed his head in recognition, then hastily completed his sweeping and ducked back inside.

A man carrying two wooden buckets emerged from an alley and looked cautiously around. Assured there was no one in sight, he started across the street, glancing apprehensively first one way, then the other.

Sitting down in one of the pants-polished chairs in front of the saloon, I looked at the far blue mountains. In a few minutes I might be dead.

It was not a good morning to die—but what morning is? Yet in a short time two men, myself and another, would meet somewhere in this town and one of us, perhaps both of us, would die.

Mulvaney rode into the street and left his horse at the stable. He walked over to me, carrying enough guns to start a war.

"The whole kit an' kaboodle. Be here within an hour. Jolly's already in town."

A woman stood at a second-floor window looking down. She turned suddenly and left the window as if called.

"If Red cuts into this scrap," Mulvaney said, "he's mine."

"You can have him."

The man with the two buckets hurried fearfully across the street, slopping water at each step.

Sheriff Tharp had not returned. There was no sign of Pinder, Morgan Park, or Bodie Miller.

Mother O'Hara had a white tablecloth on the table and the meal looked impressive.

"You should be ashamed!" she said severely. "That girl lay awake half the night, worryin' her pretty head over you."

"Over me?"

"Worried fair sick, she is. About you and that Bodie Miller!"

The door opened then and Moira entered. Her dark hair was tied in a loose knot at the back of her neck, and her eyes looked unusually large in her pale face. She avoided my glance and it was well for me she did. It was a day when I could show no weakness, not even for her.

Chapin came in, and after him, Colonel D'Arcy. I knew him at once. Right behind them was Jake Booker. He looked smug around the eyes.

They had scarcely seated themselves when Jim Pinder came in.

"Glad to see you, Jim," I said, and could see the shock of the words reflected in his eyes. "We've been fighting somebody else's battle."

He stood with his hands on his hips, looking around the room. Chapin he knew, D'Arcy he had heard about. If he knew Booker there was no evidence of it.

Turning my head, I looked at Booker. "This is a peace conference, Booker. The fighting in this area ends today."

He looked at me, his eyes blinking slowly. He was a thin-faced man with the skin tight across his cheekbones. He was disturbed, I could see that. He was a man who liked to know a little bit more about what was happening than anyone else. And this was a surprise, and as yet he had not decided what to make of it.

"I ain't said nothing about peace," Pinder said flatly. "I come in because I figured you were ready to sell."

"No—no sale. The ranch is mine. I mean to keep it. But we are organizing a peace move. Key Chapin and Sheriff Tharp are in it. Chapin has lined up the town's merchants and businessmen.

"You can come in or you can stay out, but if you don't join us you'll have to buy supplies in Silver

Reef. This town will be closed to you. Each of us in this fight will put up a bond to keep the peace, effective at daybreak tomorrow."

"You killed my brother."

"He came hunting me. That makes a difference. Look," I said, "this fight has cost you. You need money, so do we all. You sign up, or you can't ship cattle. Everybody knows you've nerve enough to face me, but what will it prove?"

He stared stubbornly at the table, but what I had said made sense, and he knew it. Finally he said, "I'll think it over. It'll take some time."

"It will take you just two minutes."

He lifted his eyes and stared hard at me. Of the two of us, he knew I was the faster man with a gun. And yet it was I who was talking peace. I knew this war had cost him heavily and no sane man would want to continue it.

Suddenly his mouth twisted in a wry sort of grin. Reluctantly, he shrugged. "You ride a man hard, Brennan. But peace it is."

"Thanks." My hand went out. He looked at it, then accepted it. Katie O'Hara filled his cup.

He looked at the coffee, then at me. "I've got to make a drive. The only way with water is across your place."

"What's wrong with that? Just so it doesn't take you more than a week to get 'em across."

The door opened and Fox came in, supporting Canaval. He was pale and drawn, but his eyes were alert and interested.

"Miss Moira could sign for me. She's the owner," he said. "But I'm for peace."

"You sign, too," I insisted. "We want to cover every thing."

Jake Booker had been taking it all in, wary and a little uncertain of what to think.

Now he decided to speak. "This is utter nonsense,

as you all know. Both ranches belong to me. You have twenty-four hours to yield possession."

Sheriff Tharp had come into the room as Booker spoke. He sat down, saying nothing. He took out his pipe with deliberation. He was an old man, but a careful man, and shrewd.

"We aren't moving, Booker. And you'll never move us."

"Are you threatening me?" He was vastly pleased that the sheriff had heard.

Ignoring the question, I made a point of filling my cup, stalling a little.

"On what basis does your claim to the Boxed M rest?"

"Bill of sale," he said promptly. "The ranch was deeded to Jay Collins, the gunfighter. Collins was killed. Collins' nephew inherited. I bought the Boxed M from him, and all appurtenances thereto."

Canaval looked at me. He smiled a little, and nodded, "So that was why."

"Jake," I said, "let me introduce you to Jay Collins."

Booker looked at Canaval as I gestured toward him. He looked and his face went two shades whiter. He started to speak, but the words stumbled and took no form. He tried to find the words and they would not come out. But any one could see that he did not doubt what I said was true. Undoubtedly Canaval tied in with what he had known of Collins.

Moira was staring at Canaval, and he looked over at her and smiled. "That's why I knew so much about your mother. She was the only person I really loved—until I met my niece."

"Mother told me about you, but I never thought—"

Turning my eyes away from her, I looked across the table at Booker. In a matter of minutes half his plan had come to nothing, and I knew that in this case half was almost as good as all.

Yet Booker was searching desperately for a way out.

He knew we would not be bluffing, that if the claim we made for Canaval was tested in court it would stand up.

He looked down at his ands, and I could almost feel his thoughts.

Now where? Now what?

TWENTY-THREE

IT WAS A SHOWDOWN, BUT FROM HERE on I was working in the dark. Counting on the shock of what I had just told him, I hoped he would believe that I knew more than I did. What I was about to say I was sure was true, but I had no proof.

"As for the Two-Bar, I've witnesses and my claim will stand in court." So much was possible, at least. Now—"Not that it will matter to you, Booker."

He was worried now, as I wanted him to be. He was not sure what I was holding back. The fact that Jay Collins was alive was an eventuality to which he had given no thought.

He looked up at me, his eyes veiled. But there was a little tic at the corner of his eye that betrayed his nervousness.

"What do you mean by that?"

"You'll hang, Booker. For murder."

Nobody said anything. Booker inhaled sharply, but he gave no other indication. He did not even protest, he just waited.

"You killed Rud Maclaren because Park's way was too slow for you. You also killed one of Slade's men from ambush.

"We can trail your horse to the scene of that crime,

Booker, and if you believe the western jury won't take the word of an Apache tracker, you're wrong."

Jake Booker straightened in his chair. He glanced around the room and found no friendliness there, but he was not a man who relied on friendships.

"Lies," he said, with a wave of dismissal, "all lies. I knew Maclaren only by sight. I had no reason to kill the man—and no opportunity."

Canaval looked doubtfully at me. Tharp was merely waiting, but a little impatiently now. If there was any one there who believed in me it was only Mulvaney.

The room was still. I could hear the clock ticking, and Katie O'Hara was standing in the door of her kitchen listening.

I felt their eyes on me, and knew the spot I was in. Yet I was sure. Carefully, I began to build. I knew that if they were to be convinced, it must be now. If Booker left this room he would escape. If I failed to prove my point, the peace we had planned would fall through.

"How Booker got him out of the house, I do not know. Probably on some pretext. Perhaps to show him the silver, perhaps to show him something I was planning.

"The mere fact that Booker, whom Maclaren knew only by reputation, would ride all that way to talk in secret would be enough to get Maclaren out.

"It does not matter what excuse was used. Booker shot him, loaded him on a horse and carried the body to my place. Then he shot Maclaren again, hoping the shot would draw me into the vicinity so I would leave tracks around the body."

Moira was watching me closely now, and Tom Fox had moved up beside me, looking across the table at Booker. Two other Boxed M hands had shifted, one to the outer door, one to a place behind Jake Booker.

Nobody seemed aware of the moves but Booker

and myself. Sweat broke out on his brow. His eyes shifted to Will Tharp, but if the sheriff noticed he did not indicate it.

"Arnold D'Arcy had found the silver lode and filed a claim. Morgan Park trailed D'Arcy to kill him. He was fiercely jealous, as we all know, but that was the least of it. Sooner or later Arnold D'Arcy would see him and would realize who he was.

"To be recognized meant arrest and trial. Following D'Arcy led him to the silver, and after the murder Morgan Park stood within reach of enough money to take him to South America to live in style.

"But he must have realized that he dared not connect his name with that of D'Arcy. Arnold had filed on the claim. He could do nothing until the assessment work lapsed, and even then to take up the claim of a man who had disappeared, and when investigation might establish a connection, was a risk he dared not take."

Supposition, much of it, but the only logic that would fit the facts.

So as the hot morning drew on into a hotter day, I built the case I had. Not much evidence, but logic enough.

Unable to make use of his discovery, Morgan Park had gone to Booker. The lawyer could find a buyer, keep Park's name out of it, and if the two ranches could be obtained, the claims might even be worked in secret. D'Arcy had evidently bribed the recorder to let out no word of the discovery.

Morgan Park had been content to work along with Rud Maclaren, believing he would sooner or later win out. But he had kept in touch with Jim Pinder.

To this Pinder acknowledged with a short nod.

And then into this stewing pot of conflicting issues and desires, I stepped.

By joining Ball I had upset the balance of power and made the certainty of the Two-Bar falling into other hands extremely doubtful.

Morgan Park still believed he could win. He was a man who had not been beaten, and he was confident. Jake Booker had been less so. Although Booker had, in my presence, doubted any belief that I had been implicated in the shooting of Lyell, he actually believed I had. The idea was upsetting.

Booker wanted the claims for himself. There was a chance that Morgan Park might be killed or arrested. Booker was already delving into Park's past, knowing there must be some reason for his great secrecy.

The assessment work D'Arcy had done on the claims had long since lapsed, but Morgan Park had dared not file on them and risk questions. The silver claims lay on land claimed by both the Two-Bar and the Boxed M, but if both ranches could be had . . .

"Lies." Booker was composed now. He was fighting for his life and he knew it, yet he was lawyer enough to see that I had little evidence.

Tom Fox was a lean, tough man. He leaned over the table.

"Some of us are satisfied, Booker," he said quietly. "Have you got any arguments that will answer a rope?"

Booker's face thinned down. "The law will protect me. Tharp's here . . . and no jury on earth will convict me on that evidence. As for the track you say you found? How do you know it hasn't been wiped out?"

I didn't know. Neither did anybody else. Canaval looked at me, and so did Tharp. There was nothing I could say to that.

"Aw, turn him loose!" Fox said carelessly. "We all know he's a crook. But turn him loose. Rud Maclaren was a good boss, and I was with Canaval when he found that track. I ain't no 'Pache, but I can read sign. Just you turn him loose. There's a mighty nice pin oak down the road a piece."

Jake Booker spread his fingers on the table. He was a frightened man. Argument and evidence might stand with Tharp, with Chapin, with Canaval, and with me. He knew he had no argument to reply to Fox.

Fox turned to the man at the door. "Joe, get an extry horse. We'll be needin' it."

Tharp began to fill his pipe. Nobody else said anything or moved. Then Key Chapin leaned back in his chair. The chair creaked a little, and Booker shifted his weight, looking up quickly at Fox.

Nothing I had said had moved Booker to more than contempt. For nothing I had said would stand up in court against the artifice Booker could bring to bear. But Fox was doing what I could not have done. Booker had looked into the eyes of Fox and there was certainty there.

A boot track to a skilled reader of sign is as good as a signature.

Jake Booker was a plotter and a conniver. He was not a courageous man. Will Tharp has said nothing. Chapin had obviously washed his hands of the situation. I was letting Fox do the talking. And Jake Booker was frightened.

The rest of us might bluff, but never Fox. The rest of us might relent, but not Fox. Booker's mouth twitched and his face was wet with sweat.

"No . . . no."

He looked around at us. He looked at me. "You can't let him hang me. Not without a trial."

"Did Maclaren have a trial?"

Booker shifted his hands on the table. He knew there was a man behind him. And Fox was across from him. And nobody was doing anything.

"Morgan Park killed him," Booker said. "It wasn't me."

He was talking. Once started, he might continue. It had not been Park, and we all knew it now.

"Where is Park?"

"Dead . . . Park killed his horse getting away. He came up to that Apache tracker of Pinder's. The Apache had a good black. Morgan Park knocked him off the horse when the Apache wouldn't trade ... the Indian shot him out of the saddle."

"You saw it?" D'Acy asked.

"Yes ... you'll find his body in a gully west of Bitter Flats. Park had started for the Reef."

Booker sat very still, waiting for us, but we did not speak. He shifted uneasily. Tharp would say nothing, and Booker knew that if he left here now he would be taken by Fox and the Boxed M riders. After that there was only the short ride to a tree.

"Tell us the truth," Chapin said finally. "If you get a trial you will have a chance."

"If I confess?" His voice was bitter. "What chance would I have then?"

"You'll live a few weeks, anyway," I said brutally. "What chance have you now?"

He sat back in his chair. "I've nothing to confess," he said. "It was Morgan Park."

Will Tharp got up from his chair. "You asked me here to conclude a peace meeting. The Boxed M, Two-Bar, and CP agree on peace, is that right?"

We all assented, and he nodded with satisfaction. "Good ... now I've some business in the northern part of the county. I'll be gone for three days."

It took a minute for Booker to grasp the idea that he was being abandoned. He looked up, his eyes shifting quickly. The man behind him eased his weight and a board creaked.

Key Chapin got up. He extended a hand to Canaval. "Be glad to help you across the street, Canaval." He turned his head to Moira. "Coming?"

She got up. Katie O'Hara had disappeared. Jim Pinder, a wry grin on his face, got up, too.

They started for the door and Jake Booker looked wildly about. Fox was across from him, smiling. Behind him was the other Boxed M hand. Outside the door with an extra horse was still another.

"*Wait!*"

Booker jumped to his feet. His face was yellow-white and he looked ghastly.

"Tharp! You can't do this! You can't leave me!"

"Why not? I've no business with you!"

"But . . . but the trial? What about the trial?"

Tharp shrugged. "What trial? We haven't evidence enough to hold you. You said that yourself." He turned away. "You're not my business now, Booker."

Fox had drawn his gun. The Boxed M hand behind Booker grabbed him suddenly. I stepped back, my hands at my sides.

"Wait a minute! Tharp—

The sheriff was outside, but he was holding the door open. The others were on the walk near him.

"Tharp! I did it. I'll talk."

There was a tablet on which Katie O'Hara wrote up her menus. I took it down, and put the inkwell beside it, and a pen.

"Write it," I said.

He hesitated, looking down. His hands trembled and he looked sick.

"All right," he said.

He sat down when the Boxed M hand released him, and Tharp returned to the room. He looked over at me and we waited, standing around, while the pen scratched steadily.

Jonathan Benaras appeared in the door. "Bodie Miller's gone," he said. "Left town."

Moira was still standing on the walk outside. The others had gone. I opened the door and stepped out.

"You're going back to the Two-Bar?" she asked.

"Even a killer has to have a home."

She looked up quickly. "Matt, don't hold that against me."

"You said what you thought, didn't you?"

I started to put my foot in the stirrup, but she looked too much like a little girl who had been spanked. "Did you ever start that trousseau?" I asked suddenly.

"Yes, but—

I dropped the reins of the horse Benaras had led up for me."

"Then we'll be married without it."

Suddenly we were both laughing like fools and I was kissing her there on the street where all of Hattan's Point could see us. People had come from saloons and stores and they were standing there grinning at us, so I kissed her again.

Then I let go of her and stepped into the saddle. "Tomorrow noon," I said, "I'll be back."

And so I rode again from Hattan's Point.

TWENTY-FOUR

Did you ever feel so good the world seemed like your big apple? That was how I felt then.

We had our showdown, and we had peace between the three ranches. We could live together now, and we could make our acres fertile and make our cattle fat.

There was grass on the range, water in the creeks, and the house I had built would have the woman it needed to make it home. From the smoke of battle I had built a home and won a wife. The world was mine.

Morgan Park was dead ... he had died in violence as he had lived, died from striking the wrong man, heedless of others, believing that his strength would pull him through. Only an Apache had fired from the ground and the bullet had torn through his skull.

I would go home now. I would make ready the house for the wife I was to have, I would care for my horses in the corral, and I would change my clothes and ride back to town to become a bridegroom.

The trail to the Two-Bar swung around a mesa and opened out on a wide desert flat, and far beyond I could see the pinnacles of the badlands beyond Dry Mesa.

A rabbit burst from the bush and sprinted off across the sage, and then the trail dipped down into a hollow, with junipers growing in and around it. And there in the middle of the road was Bodie Miller.

He was standing with his hands on his hips laughing, and there was a devil in his eyes. Off to one side of the road was Red, holding their horses.

Miller's hair was uncut and hung over the collar of his shirt. The hairs at the corners of his upper lip seemed longer and darker. But the two guns tied down to his thighs were nothing to smile about.

"Too bad to cut down the big man just when he's ridin' highest."

The horse I rode was skittish and unacquainted with me. I'd no idea how he'd stand for shooting, and I wanted to be on the ground. But there was little time. Bodie was confident, but he did not know but what I might have company further back along the road.

Suddenly I slapped spurs to the gelding and when he sprang at Bodie, I went off the other side. Hitting the ground, I ran two steps and drew as I saw Bodie's hands blur.

His guns came up and I felt mine buck in my fist. Our bullets crossed each other, although mine got off a shade the faster despite that instant of hesitation to make sure my bullet would shoot true.

His slug ripped a furrow across the top of my shoulder that stung like a million needles, but my own bullet struck him in the chest and he staggered, his eye wide and shocked.

Suddenly the devil of eagerness was in me. I was

mad, mad as I had never been before. Guns up and blasting, I started for him.

"What's the matter? Don't you like it?"

I was yelling as I walked, my guns blasting and the lead ripping into and through him.

"Now you know how the others felt, Bodie. It's an ugly thing to die because some punk wants to prove he's tough. And you aren't tough, Bodie, just a mean, nasty kid."

He swayed on his feet, bloody and finished. He was a slighter man than I, the blood staining his shirt crimson, his mouth ripped wider by a bullet. His face was gray and slashed across by the streak left by the bullet.

He stared at me, but he did not speak. Something kept him upright, but he was gone and I could see it. He stood there in the white hot sunlight and stared into my face, the last face he would ever see.

"I'm sorry, Bodie. Why didn't you stick to punching cows?"

He backed up a slow step and the gun slid from his fingers. He tried once to speak, but his lips were unable to shape the words, and then his knees buckled and he went down.

Standing over his body I looked at Red. The cowhand seemed unable to believe his eyes. He stared at Bodie Miller's used-up body, and then he lifted his eyes to me.

"I'll ride . . . just give me a chance."

"You've got it."

He swung into the saddle, then looked back at Bodie. He studied him, as if awakening from a dream.

"He wasn't so tough, was he?"

"Nobody is," I said, "especially with a slug in his belly."

He rode away then and I stood there in the lonely afternoon and saw Bodie Miller dead at my feet.

It wasn't in me to leave him there, and I did not

want to find him there when I returned. There was a gully off the trail, a little hollow where water had washed before finding a new way. So I rolled him in and shoved the banks in on top of him and then piled on some stones.

Sitting in the shade of a juniper I put together a cross, and on an old wagon tail-gate that had laid beside the road for a long time, I carved out the words:
words:

HE PLAYED OUT HIS HAND
1881

It was not much of an end for a man, but Bodie was not much of a man.

Beside some campfire Red might talk, someday, somewhere. Sooner or later the story might travel, but it would take time, and I wanted no more reputation as a gunfighter. There had been too much of that.

There was a stinging in my shoulder, but only from cut skin. At the ranch I could care for that. And it was time I was getting on.

Ahead of me the serrated ridges of the wild lands were stark and lonely against the late afternoon sky. The sun setting behind me was picking out the peak points to touch them with gold. The afternoon was gone and now I was riding home to my own ranch, riding home with the coolness of evening coming on ... and tomorrow was my wedding day.

ABOUT THE AUTHOR

LOUIS L'AMOUR, born Louis Dearborn L'Amour of French-Irish stock, is a descendant of François René, Vicompte de Chateaubriand, noted French writer, statesman, and epicure. Although Mr. L'Amour claims his writing began as a "spur-of-the-moment thing," prompted by friends who relished his verbal tales of the West, he comes by his talent honestly. A frontiersman by heritage (his grandfather was scalped by the Sioux), and a universal man by experience, Louis L'Amour lives the life of his fictional heroes. Since leaving his native Jamestown, North Dakota, at the age of fifteen, he's been a longshoreman, lumberjack, elephant handler, hay shocker, flume builder, fruit picker, and an officer on tank destroyers during World War II. And he's written four hundred short stories and over fifty books (including a volume of poetry).

Mr. L'Amour has lectured widely, traveled the West thoroughly, studied archaeology, compiled biographies of over one thousand Western gunfighters, and read prodigiously (his library holds more than two thousand volumes). And he's watched thirty-one of his westerns as movies. He's circled the world on a freighter, mined in the West, sailed a dhow on the Red Sea, been shipwrecked in the West Indies, stranded in the Mojave Desert. He's won fifty-one of fifty-nine fights as a professional boxer and pinch-hit for Dorothy Kilgallen when she was on vacation from her column. Since 1816, thirty-three members of his family have been writers. And, he says, "I could sit in the middle of Sunset Boulevard and write with my typewriter on my knees; temperamental I am not."

Mr. L'Amour is re-creating an 1865 Western town, christened Shalako, where the borders of Utah, Arizona, New Mexico, and Colorado meet. Historically authentic from whistle to well, it will be a live, operating town, as well as a movie location and tourist attraction.

Mr. L'Amour now lives in Los Angeles with his wife Kathy, who helps with the enormous amount of research he does for his books. Soon, Mr. L'Amour hopes, the children (Beau and Angelique) will be helping too.

BANTAM'S #1
ALL-TIME BESTSELLING AUTHOR
AMERICA'S FAVORITE WESTERN WRITER

☐ HIGH LONESOME	10450	$1.50
☐ TREASURE MOUNTAIN	10542	$1.50
☐ SACKETT'S LAND	10552	$1.50
☐ THE FERGUSON RIFLE	10618	$1.50
☐ KILLOE	10765	$1.50
☐ CONAGHER	10767	$1.50
☐ NORTH TO THE RAILS	10791	$1.50
☐ THE MAN FROM SKIBBEREEN	10798	$1.50
☐ SILVER CANYON	10822	$1.50
☐ MOJAVE CROSSING	10838	$1.50
☐ REILLY'S LUCK	10845	$1.50
☐ GUNS OF THE TIMBERLAND	10895	$1.50
☐ HANGING WOMAN CREEK	10896	$1.50
☐ FALLON	10897	$1.50
☐ UNDER THE SWEETWATER RIM	10901	$1.50
☐ MATAGORDA	10902	$1.50
☐ DARK CANYON	10905	$1.50
☐ THE CALIFORNIOS	10906	$1.50

Buy them at your local bookstore or use this handy coupon for ordering: